I0729198

PETAL PLUCKER

Funny, charming, and utterly captivating! I devoured this sparkling read.

— ANNIKA MARTIN, NEW YORK TIMES
BESTSELLING AUTHOR

Petal Plucker was funny, entertaining, fresh and fan-yourself-worthy . . . Their enemies-to-lovers romance is both charming, tender and steamy, and you'll love both of these characters (and their families!) and their sigh-worthy happily ever after.

— MARY DUBÉ, CONTEMPORARILY EVER
AFTER

Morland has created a masterpiece of a romance . . . one of my favorite [books] of the year.

— CRISTIINA READS

Humorous, raunchy, and refreshing, Petal Plucker has rightfully earned its way, in my opinion, as one of the best romantic comedy [books] this year.

— CAROL, TIL THE LAST PAGE

My One and Only

This book was gripping, well written & the chemistry between the characters sizzled throughout this wonderful read.

— AMAZON REVIEW

All I Want Is You

Another heartfelt, steamy, terrific story. This is an author who really knows how to create a story that catches a reader's attention and characters that capture her heart.

— BOOKADDICT

Taking a Chance on Love

Thea and Anthony are in for a surprise when it comes to the language of the heart . . . I am in awe.

— HOPELESS ROMANTIC BLOG

Then Came You

This story really pulled all my heartstrings. This was truly a beautiful story and makes you believe there really is true love out there.

— MEME CHANELL BOOK CORNER

ALSO BY IRIS MORLAND

ROMANTIC COMEDIES

He Loves Me, He Loves Me Not

Petal Plucker

War of the roses

LOVE EVERLASTING

including

THE YOUNGERS

Then Came You

Taking a Chance on Love

All I Want Is You

My One and Only

THE THORNTONS

The Nearness of You

The Very Thought of You

If I Can't Have You

Dream a Little Dream of Me

Someone to Watch Over Me

Till There Was You

I'll Be Home for Christmas

HERON'S LANDING

Seduce Me Sweetly

Tempt Me Tenderly

Desire Me Dearly

Adore Me Ardently

IF I CAN'T HAVE YOU

THE THORNTONS

IRIS MORLAND

BLUE VIOLET PRESS LLC

For my mom.

IF I CAN'T HAVE YOU

Abby shook her head as she watched her mother Fiona depart Fair Haven Memorial, where Abby worked as a nurse. She never lied to her mother, but this one little white lie was totally worth it if Abby could avoid another one of Fiona's horrific blind dates.

She winced a little as she thought about the man she'd chosen as her fake boyfriend. Mark Thornton! Of all the men in Fair Haven, Washington, it was his name that had popped into her head.

When Fiona had told Abby that she'd set her up on a blind date *again*, Abby had panicked. She'd lied to her mother and said that she was dating Mark. Fiona had bought the lie, and now Abby had to figure out how to tell her mother that they weren't a couple. They weren't even friends, for Christ's sake.

Why Mark? It's because he's my patient right now, she reasoned. He was on her mind for a good reason.

Not because he fascinated her despite his surly personality.

"Abby, I just finished with Mark Thornton," Dr. Perry Smythe told her in his barking tones.

Dr. Smythe had a tendency to yell everything he said, even though he was, in fact, one of the nicest people Abby had ever met. He just had a voice that carried.

"Do you need me to do anything else with him?" she asked.

Dr. Smythe handed her Mark's chart, pushing his too-loose glasses up his beaky nose. Dr. Smythe looked to be of an indeterminate age. At times, he looked thirty; other times, he looked closer to sixty. He was actually hedging toward fifty, if Abby remembered right. He'd run the emergency department at Fair Haven Memorial for close to twenty years now.

"No, I told him he's free to go. Tell Janine that she can clean his room." Dr. Smythe considered her. "He asked about you, though."

Abby stilled. "He did?"

"Asked if you were coming back to see him. I told him you had work to do."

She couldn't stop herself from smiling, although it was more of an incredulous smile. "Interesting. Well, maybe he wanted to be rude to me again."

"What?" Dr. Smythe's exclamation practically shook the windows.

"It's nothing." Abby shrugged. "He's not the nicest patient. Anyway, no harm, no foul. I'll see you later."

Even though Dr. Smythe didn't press the matter, he was normally very protective of his staff. They received all kinds of patients—nice ones, mean ones, crazy ones—and he did his level best to keep his staff from any abuse.

Why had Mark asked about her? She frowned. He was a weird guy. She couldn't make him out at all. One moment, he was insulting her, and then the next moment, he wanted to see her. *He must be a sadist*, she thought.

She told Janine that Mark's room was available. Before she started her rounds, she needed some coffee. When she pulled out her wallet to see if she had any cash, she realized that she didn't have her phone.

Shit! She must've left it somewhere on her rounds. When was the last time she'd had it?

She thought backward, remembering that she'd had it in her hand when she last saw Mark. Of course, she thought with an inward eye roll. All roads led back to Mark Thornton, apparently.

Entering Mark's room, she glanced around for her missing phone.

"Looking for this?"

Abby jumped, barely stifling a yelp. There was Mark Thornton, with her phone in his hand.

"Why are you still here?" she asked. She moved to grab her phone, but he didn't let her have it.

"I wanted to ask you something," was his gruff reply.

"Great. What do you want now?" She didn't care that she was being rude to a patient. Sometimes a person could only take so much abuse.

Mark Thornton had insulted her, snapped at her, and had driven her to distraction for months now. She had no interest in whatever game he wanted to play.

He stood up. Even with his arm in a sling, his face pale and wan, he managed to look imposing. Handsome.

Obnoxious.

"When exactly did we start dating?" he asked. He almost

seemed bored as he asked the question, like women were always lying about being his girlfriend.

Abby froze. She looked into those eyes of his and wondered if this was exactly how deer felt when they crossed paths with a hunter.

Like he'd leveled a target right at her heart.

"What are you talking about?" She kept her voice level from many years of practice. "How many Vicodin did you take?"

"I heard you."

She widened her eyes. "I have no idea what you're talking about. Now, can I have my phone back? Or will I have to call security on you?"

"No." He handed her the phone.

Pocketing it, she stared up at him. He was the definition of inscrutable; he could give some people a run for their money with his poker face.

Right then, she noticed that although his eyes were dark, they were actually a very dark green. Midnight green. *That's not a color, idiot,* she told herself, but it fit somehow.

Like the color of the forest right as the moon rises in the sky.

"Okay, well, thanks for giving me my phone back. I need to get back to work."

He didn't blink as he said, "I want you to do something for me."

"Do something for you?"

"Because you said I was your boyfriend. I'm assuming whoever you lied to wouldn't like that you lied. Right? So, in order for me to keep your secret from getting out, I want you to come home with me."

His expression didn't change. He could've been talking about the weather for all Abby knew.

Outrage coursed through her, and it took every ounce of her self-control not to slap Mark across his handsome face.

"I'm not having sex with you to get you to keep your mouth shut!" she hissed. She pointed a finger at him. "You, sir, are a pig. How dare you proposition me? Or blackmail me? Or whatever term you want to use? Do you need sex that badly that you'd stoop to—"

He pressed her lips closed with his thumb and forefinger. His eyes were dark now, his eyes narrowed.

"I'm not propositioning you," he said, disgust lacing his tone. "Why the hell would you think that?"

She pushed his hand away, rubbing her lips. She didn't want to think about why her body tingled from that random touch.

"Then why else do you want me to go home with you?" Now she was just confused.

Mark rubbed the back of his neck. "I need someone to help me on the ranch. With this broken arm, I can't do everything myself like I used to. I need someone to come out and give me a hand."

Abby almost laughed. Actually, she did laugh: giggles erupted from her throat, and she clapped a hand to her mouth.

"You want me to—what?—throw hay bales around? What makes you think I'd be a person who could even do that?" Just thinking about doing ranch work—fixing fences? brushing down horses? what did you do on a ranch anyway?—when Abby was not exactly what anyone would call "fit," was beyond hilarious to her.

But at Mark's look, she bit the inside of her cheek to stifle any more laughter.

"I don't mean that kind of work. Obviously you aren't going to be good for that." He waved a hand at her general person.

"Yes, thank you." Her voice was wry now. "I'm aware I'm hardly big and muscular like you."

To Abby's surprise, a flush crawled up Mark's cheeks.

"No, I need you to do housework and get groceries and things like that." He raised his broken arm a little. "I live too far out to get takeout every night, and it'll take me way too long to cook with one working hand."

Abby was almost more outraged now than when she thought he'd been propositioning her for sex. "You want me to be your *maid?*"

Now he had the grace to look abashed. "No." He shook his head. "I really didn't think this over, did I? But I thought we could come to an agreement, since you need me."

"I don't need you!"

"Do you want everyone to know that you lied about being my girlfriend?"

"No, but you could just not tell anyone." She crossed her arms, trying to appear forceful. "You could keep your mouth shut. It might be fun for you for once."

He shrugged. "It's no skin off of my nose to tell people you made this story up about us."

Gritting her teeth, Abby considered the pros and cons of the situation.

Pros: Her mother would leave her alone.

Cons: Everything else.

"Fine, tell everyone. You want my mom's phone number,

too? Or are you already Facebook friends?" She was totally bluffing. She wanted to stay as Mark's imaginary girlfriend because the alternative meant going on more painfully awkward dates.

The last date had been the worst out of all of them. Abby had actually thought he'd had promise, based on Fiona's description of him. "An architect!" she'd told Abby with undisguised glee. "He's behind those new apartment complexes downtown." Fiona had told Abby that Chris had a "full head of hair, a nice smile, and a way with words."

Fiona had neglected to mention that Chris was also a collector.

He'd invited Abby over for a drink, and she'd agreed, because he was nice and she didn't have anything else to do. When Chris had opened his door, though, Abby realized that Chris had a Lego collection rivaling that of Legoland itself. Lego sets filled his apartment from floor to ceiling, covering every square inch of space not used for actual furniture.

Chris had then proceeded to explain the history of every Lego set he'd put together. But it was when Chris had shown Abby the sexy Lego costume he kept for these occasions—he had said with a slow wink—that Abby had told him she had a family emergency and had run straight home.

So, yes, being Mark's maid would be infinitely preferable to living through another date like Chris again.

The present rushed back when Mark pulled out his phone and began to type something in.

"What are you doing?" she asked, apprehensive.

"Looking for your mom on Facebook. Fiona is her name, right?"

She didn't want to know how Mark knew that, and she

really didn't want him to tell Fiona a damn thing. She tried to grab his phone, but he was so tall that he only had to lift it a few inches above his head to keep it away from her.

Asshole.

"Is it really that important? That you get your mom off of your back?" He seemed genuinely curious now.

Abby sighed. Rubbing her temples, she muttered, "Yeah, it is. Does your mother set you up on dates because she's convinced you're going to die a spinster surrounded by your twenty cats?"

"No, but I don't like cats."

"Well, my mom does think that about me. And I'm tired of it. So, yes, I lied, and I don't want her to know how pathetic I am." She sighed.

His lips twisted into a slight smile. Stepping closer to her, he said in a low voice, "Come stay with me at my ranch and help me out. I'll pay you. I was going to hire someone anyway, and since you're a nurse, you can help me not screw up my arm again."

Abby considered him. She couldn't help but feel that this wasn't so much blackmail as Mark's attempt to get closer to her. Then again, she was probably reading too much into this.

He wasn't propositioning me. He just wants a maid. She felt stupid for her disappointment. If she could kick herself, she would. *He wouldn't want a* mousy nurse *like me anyway, right?*

He'd called her that at The Rise and Shine, the local bakery in Fair Haven, and the words had hurt more than she wanted to admit. Short, curvy, and this side of plain, Abby had never been all that self-confident. And her ex-boyfriend had done such a number on her self-esteem that she preferred to avoid dating.

What man would want her, anyway?

Not Mark Thornton, that was for sure.

"So if I come live in your castle—"

"Ranch."

"In your ranch-castle, and if I bake you cakes and wash your floors and do your laundry, you'll be my boyfriend?"

Abby knew it was crazy to accept this, but it would be worth it to get her mother off of her back. She couldn't go on another one of her mother's blind dates. And, she had to admit, she was intrigued despite herself. What would it be like to see Mark in his natural habitat?

His lips quirked into a small smile. "Basically, yes."

"Good. I want $50 per hour and I want my gas reimbursed. I have a job, as you know, so I'll be there at weird hours, although I usually have a day shift. I'm also bringing my cats with me."

She expected objections, but Mark shrugged. "Fine."

They shook on it, and Abby couldn't stop herself from enjoying the feeling of his callused hand against her own. He was so tall, so broad, and she couldn't stop herself from inhaling his scent.

Yes, he'd insulted her. But she was still a woman—she could look and not touch, right?

"Oh, I forgot one thing." She tipped her chin up. "This is completely platonic. No kissing, no touching, no sex, nothing. You're my boyfriend in name only."

If she weren't imagining things, she would've thought his eyes gleamed. He gave her a slow perusal that set her body aflame.

"If that's what you want," was his only reply.

"It is. Now, I'm going back to work. I'll see you Saturday morning. Does that work for you?"

"Fine."

She waited for him to say something else, like he looked forward to seeing her again. Or even that he'd come to his senses and would let her off of the hook

But he didn't say anything.

"Bye, then. And don't overdo it with that arm," she said as she walked away.

MARK WATCHED ABBY LEAVE, enjoying the rounded curve of her ass.

When she shut the door behind her, he let out a breath he hadn't even known he'd been holding. He hadn't planned on asking Abby to be his—what? Fake girlfriend? Maid? House-keeper? Friend? But when she'd come into this room, he had wanted her.

You're a special kind of stupid, aren't you? he thought.

So instead of asking Abby out like a normal man, he'd cajoled her into working for him so he'd keep his mouth shut about her little lie.

He wouldn't have told her mother about her fabrication anyway, but Abby didn't know that. And when the idea had sprung upon him, he hadn't been able to let it go.

Now, though, he was going to have to contend with Abby Davison and her round ass hanging around his ranch. An ass he was not allowed to touch.

Definitely a special kind of stupid.

He drove back to his ranch, wondering what the hell he

was going to do about this predicament. A predicament that was his own damn fault. Maybe he should tell Abby the deal was off. But then he wouldn't see her again, would he?

And he wanted to see her again.

He slammed his truck door shut when he arrived home. Inhaling the fresh air—the smell of grass, horses, and hay—his erratic heartbeat slowed some.

He may have made a deal with the devil, but he'd done it. At the very least, it would be nice to have someone other than Charlie around to talk to.

"I told you that you broke it," Charlie said as he came out of the barn toward Mark. Charlie was in his forties, a grizzled man with tufts of gray hair sprouting from his head like weeds. He had worked on farms his entire life and knew them better than he knew anything else. When Mark had gotten Charlie to agree to work with him, Mark had known he'd been lucky.

Charlie was hardly a conversationalist, though. He was rather like Mark himself; both men preferred silence over idle chatter and could go the entire day without saying more than ten words to each other.

Mark lifted his broken arm. "You were right," he said. "Do I owe you something for being right?"

Charlie laughed, a gruff sound like rocks tumbling down a ravine. "Naw, but good thing you didn't make it worse, still working after you'd broken it. Damn stupid thing to do, you know."

Mark almost laughed. If Charlie knew about his latest stupid thing...

"A woman's coming Saturday to help me out," Mark said. He didn't wait to see Charlie's reaction.

"A woman? Who? Why? Did you break your brain, too?" Charlie guffawed at that.

"No, but I can't do everything with a broken arm." *Liar*, he thought to himself. He could manage just fine without additional help, but Abby didn't know that, did she? "She's going to help around the house."

"Huh. So a maid."

Mark glared at Charlie over his shoulder. "She's not a maid."

"Okay then. A housekeeper." Charlie shrugged. "As long as she doesn't get in the way around here, or try to make us eat kale chips. What is it with women and kale, huh?"

"You're definitely asking the wrong man about how women think," was Mark's wry reply.

CHAPTER TWO

After arriving home, Abby wanted a drink and then to sleep for the rest of her life. She was beyond exhausted: not only because of her run-in with Mark, but the three patients who'd taken all her concentration and training afterward.

The worst patient had been the homeless man who had shouted at her when she wouldn't tell Dr. Smythe to get him more painkillers. He'd stumbled out of the hospital before they'd cleared him to leave. Abby knew he'd return before long.

She smiled when her two cats, Darcy and Wentworth, were at the door when she came inside. Both black cats, you could only tell them apart because Wentworth had a smudge of white on his chest. They always came to greet her when they heard her car pull up.

Wentworth stood on his hind legs, his paws on her knee, begging for an ear scratch. Darcy swished his tail, acting aloof, but when Abby scratched his chin, he started purring.

"Come on, let's go get something to eat," she said to the cats, who followed her into the kitchen. After feeding the felines, she fixed herself a plate of leftovers and decided that she'd watch some stupid reality show before turning in. Sipping her wine, she told herself to forget about what had happened today.

But even the shenanigans of some crazy brides on TV weren't enough to keep her from thinking about her deal with Mark Thornton.

"I've lost my mind," she said to Wentworth when he climbed onto her lap. "I should be committed. Or maybe Mark should be. He's off his rocker. Who does something like that?"

Wentworth purred and closed his eyes as she petted him.

Abby didn't know if Mark needed someone to help him. Maybe he did, or maybe he just wanted to screw with her. He didn't want to *screw* her, like she'd initially thought. Of course not.

She wasn't a woman to inspire insatiable lust in men, generally speaking. She didn't consider that a bad thing, per se, but sometimes it stung.

Was it so wrong to want someone to want her for once?

Her ex-boyfriend Derek had made a point to tell her he'd never really wanted her. She'd been convenient, he'd said. Abby knew he'd said that because he was pissed she'd wanted to end things; he'd wanted to hurt her, and he'd succeeded. Logically, she knew that. But emotionally? It had struck a nerve.

Who would want a fattie like you? I didn't get with you for your looks, he'd said during one particularly brutal argument.

She'd countered that if he'd found her so unattractive, why had he begged her to go on a date with him when they'd first met?

"Men are idiots," she said to no one except her cats. They were the only men in her life she trusted. At least cats were honest about only caring about themselves. She respected their unapologetic selfishness.

When her phone rang, she groaned, because only one person called her instead of texted.

"Hi Mom," she said. She knew Fiona would want to grill her more about her new (and imaginary) boyfriend.

"Oh good, you're home. I thought you had a late shift tonight." Abby could hear the excitement in Fiona's voice. "We barely got a chance to chat earlier. I want you to tell me *everything.*"

Abby almost laughed. If only she could tell Fiona everything! Her mother would sure get a kick out of her daughter having a made-up boyfriend, wouldn't she?

Guilt assailed her. She was lying, and continuing to lie. But now that she'd started this, she had to see it through to the bitter end. *Or I could tell Mark the deal's off.*

"You know the Thorntons, right?" was what Abby said instead.

"Of course I do. Although I don't know much about your Mark. What does he do? Where did you meet? When did you decide to make things official?"

Abby realized she didn't know a thing about him. She needed to rectify that if she were going to play his girlfriend.

Geez, I'm a terrible person, aren't I?

Abby told her mother what she did know about Mark,

which was not very much. When Fiona pressed for details about how they'd started dating, Abby remained coy.

"Mark doesn't like his personal business out in the open," she said. She imagined he'd agree with that statement.

"Oh, come on! Don't be like that. I've been waiting for this ever since you and Derek broke up. I was afraid you'd never date again. I know your breakup was hard on you—"

"Let's not talk about Derek right now." Abby looked down at Wentworth, whose eyes were slits, like he were judging her. "Actually, I wanted to let you know that I'll be living with Mark for a time to help him, since he broke his arm."

Abby didn't know how Fiona would react to that announcement. Dismay, excitement? Disapproval? But when Fiona let out an ear-splitting scream, Abby had to hold the phone away from her ear.

"You're moving in with him? Already? I can't believe it!" Fiona cried. "You should've told me right away!"

"It's not like that—it's temporary. He asked me to help him."

"Doesn't matter! This is a big step for you, although it does seem fast. Are you sure about this?"

No, I'm not sure about much of anything anymore. "Oh, totally sure."

After giving Fiona as many details as she could, they said goodbye, Fiona assuring Abby that this sounded like an amazing chance for her to "seal the deal."

Fiona Davison had raised Abby by herself after Abby's father had passed away when she was a small child. Abby couldn't blame her mother for wanting her to find happiness with a marriage and a family. The depressing thing was that

Abby did want a husband and children, but she had come to accept that there was little to no chance that would happen.

She finished her wine and got another glass before she got ready for bed. Lately, she avoided mirrors, but tonight, she gazed at herself without flinching. Standing there naked after her bath, she took in her light brown hair and her light brown eyes.

She looked pale, which she attributed to stress. She'd lost weight recently, although not because she'd been trying to. Turning this way and that, she looked at her breasts—overly large, in her opinion—and the curve of her belly. The stretch marks, the cellulite. She plucked a hair from a mole behind her knee.

Her ass was decent, but nothing amazing. She had nice toes, she supposed.

Darcy hopped onto the counter and butted her hand with his head. She petted him, her thoughts far away.

Two years ago, when she'd still been dating Derek, she'd thought she was pregnant because she'd missed her period for two months. She'd always had irregular periods, and although she and Derek had always used condoms, she'd wondered if one hadn't worked.

After the pregnancy test had come back negative, her doctor had done further tests to discover why her periods had disappeared. As a nurse, Abby knew a woman could stop menstruating if she were stressed, too thin, or a host of other reasons besides pregnancy.

After blood tests and an ultrasound, her doctor had told she had Polycystic Ovarian Syndrome, PCOS for short.

"It's actually very common," he'd said in his prosaic tones, "but most women haven't heard of it, unless they're diagnosed with it. Based on the cysts on your ovaries and your being overweight, I would be surprised if you could get pregnant naturally at all. You also have a bicornuate uterus, meaning that it's heart-shaped. That will make it even more difficult to conceive. If you do get pregnant, there's double the chance of miscarriage as well. Diet and exercise, plus going on the Pill, are our best course of action for now."

Abby had found it ironic that, even though she was a nurse, she'd never thought she had something wrong with her. She'd heard of PCOS before, but she'd never studied it extensively.

It had been surreal, hearing those words said in the same way you'd say, *There's a sale on potatoes at the store* or *I need a ride to work tomorrow morning.* Her dreams of having a family someday, dashed in an instant. Although her diagnosis wasn't a definitive one, her doctor hadn't seemed hopeful.

Abby had returned home, devastated and terrified, and she'd cried the rest of the evening.

Derek had been sympathetic, to a degree. She'd seen the look in his eyes when she'd told him about her inability to have children. He hadn't said the words, but after that, their relationship had never recovered. Suddenly, the dreams of the future had shattered, until everything had fallen apart.

I want to be with a woman who can have kids, Derek had told her that last day. *Sorry, Abby. I don't want to adopt some other people's kids, either. You know what I mean, right?*

After her mirror perusal, Abby got dressed for bed and crawled underneath the covers. She almost couldn't blame Derek. Her body couldn't do what it should do. She knew she was more than a body made to carry a baby, but the hurt pierced her heart anyway.

She was abnormal. *Broken.*

She hadn't told Fiona about her diagnosis. It would've hurt her too much. And although Abby knew that ignoring a diagnosis was hardly the best course of action, she preferred not to think about it. If she didn't think about it, maybe it wasn't real.

It was good that Mark didn't want her, she decided. Because what were the chances he'd stay with her if he discovered the truth?

He might not be as cruel as Derek, but she'd see the shadow in his eyes. The disappointment. The judgment.

It was better this way, she told herself as she tried to fall asleep.

"Shit, what did you do to yourself?" Caleb asked, seeing Mark's arm. "Did you get run over by a tractor?"

"Hilarious. No, I got thrown from my horse."

Caleb's eyes widened. "Damn, man, be careful. You're lucky it wasn't your neck."

Mark grunted, agreeing with his older brother's assessment but not wanting to admit it. He'd been stupid, riding a horse that still needed training. But he'd assumed his experience would outweigh a touchy horse's predilection for getting spooked.

"Glad you're okay," Harrison, the eldest Thornton brother, said as he handed Mark a beer. "How long do you have to wear a cast?"

"Six weeks, give or take. The break was clean."

Mark chatted with his brothers before they all went into

the dining room in Caleb and Megan's new house. Megan had insisted on having everyone over to celebrate the move.

"Everyone" included Harrison and his fiancée Sara, Caleb and his girlfriend Megan, and Jubilee, the youngest Thornton. Megan owned The Rise and Shine, the local bakery downtown, and she liked to experiment with her cuisine. Based on the amazing smells wafting from the kitchen, dinner would be a hit.

Mark couldn't stop himself from feeling like a third wheel, despite his brothers' best efforts to include him in the conversation. He listened to a lot of chatter about Sara and Harrison's upcoming wedding, and how Caleb and Megan enjoyed living together.

He also couldn't stop the curl of envy in his gut every time he looked at his brothers. They'd both fallen in love with incredible women who adored them.

Jubilee sat next to Mark, giving him a secret smile, like she knew how he felt about being single amidst all of these lovebirds.

As far as Mark knew, Jubilee hadn't dated anyone. The thought of his baby sister with a man made him want to punch somebody. Jubilee had suffered two bouts of childhood leukemia, and the family had protected her from the world as a result.

Mark sometimes had a hard time seeing Jubilee as a grown woman now. He couldn't help but remember Jubilee as a child, bald and sick, hooked up to wires and machines.

But the future marched on, even if Mark didn't want it to. Jubilee was grown; his brothers were in love; and he was still alone, like he liked it.

When Megan asked Sara if she'd decided on her wedding colors, Mark almost groaned.

Jubilee leaned over to ask, "How's Delilah?"

That made him smile. Delilah was his chestnut mare who was due to give birth with her first foal soon. He'd acquired Delilah over a year ago, and she'd become his favorite horse, mostly for her sassy personality and love of carrots.

"She's doing good. I think she'll be pretty uncomfortable soon, though, but her foal is growing as it should," he said.

"Do you know if it's a boy or a girl?"

"It's a girl."

Jubilee smiled, surprised. "Honestly, I didn't think you'd know that, but I don't know anything about horses. Aw, Mark, you're going to have a little girl."

Mark tugged on Jubilee's braid, rather like he did when they were kids.

"Who's having a girl?" Megan asked from across the table. "Are we talking about human girls or some other species?"

"We're talking about horses," Jubilee replied. "Mark's horses, specifically."

"You're having a baby horse? Oh, when? I want to see a baby horse!" Megan looked enchanted by the idea.

"It's called a foal," Caleb said, which earned him a stuck-out tongue and a threat to keep his big mouth shut if he didn't want to pay for it later.

The group peppered Mark with questions, which he didn't mind answering. He'd begun breeding horses two years ago, but Delilah was something special. Multiple breeders had wanted to breed their stallions to her, and Mark had a distinct feeling she'd bring him quite a lot of money in the end. But

Mark had waited until Delilah was a little older, and this year was the first time she'd be foaling.

"I'd love to come out sometime to see your ranch," Sara said. "James, too." James was Sara's six-year-old son from her previous marriage.

"Oh man, can you imagine James riding a horse?" Megan laughed. "He'd never get off of it!"

"I don't give riding lessons," Mark said.

When Harrison raised an eyebrow at him, he could've bitten his tongue in half. He didn't mean to sound like an asshole, at least most of the time.

"I mean, I don't know much about teaching kids," he explained to Sara.

Sara didn't look offended; instead, she smiled at him. "I wouldn't want to try to keep James away from horses, either, even if he'd probably get kicked within five minutes."

Everyone laughed, the brief tension dispelled.

When Megan mentioned that she'd talked to Abby recently, Mark couldn't stop himself from listening to Megan's every word. He almost expected Megan to call him out about his deal with Abby. But Megan never alluded it. *Abby didn't tell her*, he thought.

He let out a relieved breath. Jubilee gave him a questioning look. He ignored it.

He knew this arrangement between him and Abby was a terrible idea. And what did he hope would come of it? That Abby would decide that she liked him? He almost laughed at himself.

Mark had wanted her to be near him. It was stupid, and selfish, and he was an asshole. Yet he couldn't find the strength to call it off.

It was ironic, he thought wryly, that he'd decided to pursue a woman at all when he'd vowed to keep to himself after his last relationship. His ex, Tina, had stomped on his heart without blinking.

Mark had fallen hard for Tina Gage when he'd first seen her in college. With her auburn hair and laughing eyes, she'd shone the brightest in every room she'd entered. He'd fallen hard and fast. When he'd asked her out and she'd said yes, he could hardly believe it. By the third month of dating, he'd known he was in love with her.

And then she'd cheated on him—with his best friend.

Mark forced the memory away, but the cake Megan had baked tasted like ash in his mouth. He could barely finish it.

After Tina, Mark had sworn off love. What was love except manipulation? A means to control someone? Tina had led him around by the nose, and he'd told himself never again.

An hour later, Mark said his goodbyes and headed out to his truck. To his surprise, Harrison followed him, calling his name.

"Hey, everything all right? You were quiet in there."

Mark grunted. "Am I ever chatty?"

Harrison grinned. He looked a lot like Mark, although he wasn't as broad-shouldered. Harrison was a pediatric oncologist who owned his own practice in Fair Haven.

"Good point." Harrison slapped him on the shoulder, his eyes filled with concern. "It's been good seeing more of you lately. Don't hide out at that ranch of yours too much, okay? Sara and I are always happy to have you over."

Mark almost told his brother about Abby. What would

Harrison think about this scenario? He'd think he was crazy, for one.

Mark had always been the black sheep of the family. He loved his siblings, but he'd set himself apart from them since childhood. As an adult, he'd managed on his own without complaint.

"I'm fine. See you later." Mark got into his truck, trying not to notice the hurt on Harrison's face in his rearview window.

CHAPTER THREE

"You'll need to stay off your foot for the next few weeks. It's a pretty bad sprain, but luckily, nothing was broken." Abby's latest patient was a ten-year-old boy who'd sprained his ankle after his friends had dared him to climb a tree.

The boy nodded, his mother giving him a look of exasperation. "What did I say about doing dares?" she exclaimed. "You'll break your neck someday!"

"I didn't break my neck, though," the boy replied.

Abby bit back a smile. After speaking to the mother about her son's aftercare, Abby glanced at the clock outside in the hallway. Almost lunchtime. Had four hours already passed since she'd arrived? She'd been working nonstop today and hadn't even gotten a chance to have a cup of coffee.

You never knew what would happen in the ER on any given day. Some days, it was a ghost town, and then on other days, it was like the entire town decided to have a heart attack all at once.

"Room 125 needs a blood draw," Janine said as she

handed Abby another chart. An LPN and one of Abby's favorite coworkers, Janine was no-nonsense and always worked hard. She wasn't squeamish, and she didn't complain when she had to change bed pans or clean up various bodily fluids.

"Thanks. What's the lowdown on this one? Possible undiagnosed diabetes?" Abby asked.

"Seems like it. He has all the symptoms: excessive urination and thirst plus the sweet-smelling urine."

Abby looked through the chart before tucking it under her arm. "Thanks. Hey, want to get lunch together today?"

"If we don't end up getting a hundred more people coming in here today, sure," Janine replied with a wry look.

After Abby had done the blood draw and sent it to the laboratory for further testing, she had to stifle a yawn. Her feet hurt, and she needed something to eat. She probably had time to snag something from the cafeteria—

"I need to get a prescription," she heard a gruff voice say only a few yards away. Then: "Can I talk to the nurse at least? Abby Davison? She attended me."

Janine nodded as Mark Thornton spoke in a pained voice, his expression grim and his skin pale. What was he doing here? Had he hurt his arm again?

"I heard my name," she said as she approached the pair. "I can take over from here," she said to Janine. "I set his arm yesterday."

"I'll be down the hallway if you need me," Janine said before walking away.

"Have you re-injured yourself? You don't look good." Abby touched his forehead. No fever, which was a good sign. But a sheen of sweat covered his brow.

"No, my arm's fine." He winced. "I need that prescription again."

She raised her eyebrows. "Again? What happened to the first one?"

"I threw it away." He looked both defensive and embarrassed. She couldn't help but feel sympathetic toward this strong man who thought he could power through any pain by sheer force of will. Considering how he looked right this second, he wasn't doing too well.

She was about to scold him, but she bit her tongue. At least he'd come to his senses and accepted that he needed help.

"Here, sit down," she ordered, guiding him to a nearby chair. "How much pain are you in on a scale of one to ten?"

"Eight point five, I guess."

"Let me find the attending physician so he can write you a new script. And then you'll actually get it filled this time?"

He nodded, grimacing. "That's why I'm here."

Abby explained the situation to Dr. Smythe, who was wary about giving out another prescription for pain medication.

"Tell this patient of yours that he's lucky we were able to get him a new prescription so quickly. We can't exactly hand out narcotics like candy," Dr. Smythe said.

Abby nodded. "Thanks for this."

She returned to Mark, but before she gave him the prescription, she said, "Do you want someone to call this in now? What pharmacy do you use?"

He looked dismayed by the question; Abby had a feeling Mark very rarely went to the doctor or pharmacy. Getting Janine, Abby had her find the nearest pharmacy to fill the prescription.

Abby sat down next to Mark after explaining the situation to Janine. "Can you drive home? You shouldn't drive after taking Vicodin."

He rose from his chair, frowning down at her. "I'll be fine. Thanks for getting this done so fast."

"Of course. It's my job."

Abby wondered, not for the first time, why this man had demanded that she come stay with him. Was he lonely? She couldn't help but feel for him if that were the case. Lately, she had felt lonely too, like she was adrift with no one to throw her a rope to pull her back onto dry land.

Although acting like Mark, of all people, would be the one to throw her a rope would be ridiculous. He'd persuaded her to play housekeeper to keep her secret, hadn't he? Any man capable of that kind of manipulation was one she should stay clear of.

She wanted to ask him why he'd done it, why her, why now? She wanted to talk about what he expected her to do when she showed up on Saturday. Would he broadcast her little white lie to everyone in Fair Haven if she didn't show?

"Abby..." he said in a low voice. "I wanted to talk to you, actually—"

"Abby! There you are!"

She turned to see her ex-boyfriend, Derek striding toward her, like they were old friends running into each other.

What is it with these people showing up at my job? she thought miserably.

Derek looked handsome and happy, although Abby couldn't help but notice that he'd gained a little weight around the middle. He hadn't gotten new pants yet, and she wondered how much longer his belt would last before it finally gave out from the strain.

Derek was good-looking, but nothing above average, either. He was about five-eight, which he was sometimes self-conscious about. His best feature was his eyes—a light blue—but otherwise, he wasn't the type of person one found particularly arresting or memorable.

Not like Mark Thornton, with his dark eyes, his stormy features, his gruffness and broad shoulders. Mark was the type of man that you couldn't forget, and seeing the two men side by side, Abby couldn't help but compare them.

"What are you doing here, Derek?" she asked her ex, trying not to wonder what Mark's reaction was to this little scene.

"You look good, Abby. How are you?"

She was nonplussed and a bit irritated. She hadn't heard from Derek in the year since their break-up, and now he showed up at her work like this?

Derek embraced her. She stood stiffly, patting his shoulder before pulling away. When he placed a hand on her arm, she gritted her teeth. The only reason she didn't slap his hand away was because she didn't want to make a scene for the insatiable grapevine that was hospital gossip.

"I'm good. Busy. I need to get back to work here in a second."

"Oh, I know how busy you get." Derek winked at her—winked! "But I thought I could take you to lunch today. I've wanted to see you for a while now." His voice lowered. "Can we talk?"

She opened her mouth to tell him *hell no,* when Mark cleared his throat.

"This is Mark Thornton," she said. "This is Derek Barry. My ex-boyfriend," she made sure to add, so Derek didn't try anything stupid, like say they were still together.

Derek's eyes creased in annoyance at that dig, but he shook Mark's hand. "And how do you two know each other?"

Before Abby could respond, Mark said in his deep voice, "Abby and I are dating. She's my girlfriend."

MARK HADN'T PLANNED to say those words aloud. In fact, he'd come to the hospital not only to get another prescription, but to tell Abby that their deal was off. He'd been out of his mind yesterday.

Now, though, he wanted to rub their fake relationship in her ex's smarmy face. The way he kept trying to touch Abby when she didn't want him to? How he smiled at her in that condescending way?

Mark wanted to rearrange the asshole's face right there in the hospital lobby.

Abby stilled beside him; she looked confused and shocked. But to his relief, she didn't contradict him.

And God only knew how satisfying it was to see the look of dejection on her ex's face right then.

"I didn't know you were dating somebody," Derek said. He frowned. "How long have you been together?"

Mark was about to tell him to shove off when Abby replied, "Not long. Now, I need to get back to work." She touched Mark's arm, and the brief sensation of her fingers on his skin was enough to set him ablaze. "Can you get home all right?" she murmured.

He swallowed. "Yeah."

"Then I'll see you this weekend."

His gaze fell on her lips, his heart starting to pound. The world faded away in that moment. Before he could consider his actions, he leaned down to kiss her.

She didn't pull away, thank God. He brushed his lips across hers—a mere touch—and then he pulled away. But that simple kiss, close-mouthed and sedate, set his blood boiling. He watched as a flush crawled up Abby's cheeks, which only filled him with satisfaction.

"Bye, Abby," he rumbled. He narrowed his eyes at Derek: a silent threat.

Mess with her, and you'll deal with me.

CHAPTER FOUR

Mark had never had a woman over. Well, not at his ranch. Things with Tina had ended as he was starting the ranch, and he'd never wanted to bring any woman back with him.

Any encounters he had were in town, or on the road for business. Nothing serious, only casual. Most were one-night stands that had no expectations beyond mutual pleasure and a farewell in the morning.

Waking up right as dawn peeked over the horizon, Mark had wondered what the hell he'd gotten himself into. And how did you prepare for a woman staying at your place anyway?

He had a guest room, but no one had used it. He frowned when he realized the room smelled stale. He opened a window, changed the sheets and comforter, and then winced when he saw how bare the room was.

"Jesus Christ, this isn't a hotel," he muttered to himself.

Abby would have her own bathroom as well, which was also rarely used. He placed clean towels and toilet paper inside the cabinets, wondered for a moment about soap (didn't women have lots of different kinds of soaps?), and decided to call it a day.

If Charlie could see him now, he'd never live it down.

He didn't know when Abby would arrive, except she'd said some time Saturday morning. He realized he hadn't gotten her number. He'd need to rectify that immediately.

After his trip to the hospital, he'd picked up his painkillers, driven home, and promptly collapsed in a haze of pain meds and exhaustion. He'd told himself he was twenty times a fool for saying that they were dating to make her ex-boyfriend mad. The news that they were dating would get all over town before the week was out.

He should tell Abby the deal was off. Nobody had signed a contract. But he had a feeling if her ex discovered the relationship was a ploy, he'd be out for blood. If this lie protected Abby, so be it.

This was what he told his conscience as he stepped outside for his usual morning routine. Charlie didn't work weekends, for which he was grateful. He didn't need his ranch hand giving him looks that only proved that Mark was a total fool.

It was a beautiful fall day: crisp and clear, the leaves had already changed to colors of deep red and orange. They crunched under his boots as he made his way to the horse barn. He inhaled the sweet scent of hay.

Mark currently owned three horses, including the apple of his eye, Delilah. Delilah neighed in greeting when he came to her stall, sticking her nose out and demanding her morning nose rub.

"How's my girl?" Mark asked as he stroked the horse's velvety nose. He saw a ripple of movement inside her large, pregnant belly. Delilah was due to deliver within two months, if not sooner, and she was at the point in her pregnancy where she was getting uncomfortable.

Mark entered her stall, giving her one last nose rub before he stroked his hands down her sides. The foal inside her moved, and he could make out hooves pressing against her sides. Delilah snorted.

"I know. You're ready to have this over with, aren't you? I am, too. You've been pregnant forever."

Delilah seemed to nod in agreement. Horse gestation was longer than a human's—closer to a year rather than nine months—and Mark couldn't wait to meet this foal. He also missed being able to ride Delilah. He took her for walks around the enclosure, but it wasn't the same as riding her around his property.

After feeding and watering Delilah, he did the same for the two other horses: a young gelding named Samson and another mare named Rosemary.

He then fed and watered the goats, a rowdy bunch who always tried to munch on his pant legs. Goat's milk was in high demand, and Mark had reckoned he could make some nice extra cash by raising a few goats.

He also had about a dozen hens that provided regular eggs. Despite his brothers' teasing, he didn't own any pigs—yet. He wouldn't count out any animal that could bring in revenue.

Mark loved this time of day, when he worked with the animals and nobody bothered him. Ranch life suited him more than city life. Although Fair Haven wasn't exactly a metropolis, it still had too many people for Mark's liking.

Things were simpler here. He understood horses and chickens and goats.

People, though? They tended to be a conundrum.

It took him longer to do his usual chores with his broken arm, and he grunted and swore when he had to figure out how to do something one-handed. Things like getting a bag of feed open, or carrying something and opening a door at the same time.

By the time he finished, it was close to lunch. Abby hadn't yet arrived.

Was she not going to come at all? His gut twisted in disappointment, and then he told himself he was an idiot. *What did you think would happen? She'd come and stay with you forever?*

But his disappointment cleared when he heard a car driving down the dirt road, a car he knew was Abby's. She parked outside his house right as he approached.

"I wondered if you were coming at all," he said as she opened her car door.

He'd never seen her wearing anything but scrubs, so seeing her in jeans and a sweater seemed strange. Her hair was in some complicated braid around her head. She looked fresh and young. Pretty, if he were honest.

"Sorry, took me longer than I thought." She opened the back seat and handed him a pet carrier. Something inside yowled in protest. "Where should I put the cats?"

Cats. He'd forgotten about the cats. Didn't cats live outside? But Abby was carrying the other cat inside, so he had to assume that she wanted them to stay indoors. He frowned down at the yowling creature.

"Let me show you to your room," he said.

He couldn't see her face now, but she hadn't seemed nervous getting out of her car. Did she regret agreeing to this? Did he? He didn't know anymore. All he knew was that the thought of her not coming at all had filled him with disappointment.

Mark's house was the complete opposite of his parents' mansion, which he'd done on purpose. While his parents' place was ornate and palatial, his place was open and simple in comparison. Large windows let in lots of natural light, and the furniture was all warm earth tones. He'd wanted a house that was comfortable, not imposing.

"Nice place," Abby said, craning her head to take it all in. "It's very...bright."

"What, did you think I lived in a cave?" he asked wryly.

She grinned at him. "Maybe. You definitely growl like a bear."

He grunted as he led her into her room.

"I'll get the cats settled," she said. "They prefer to be in one room for a bit until they calm down."

She opened one carrier door, and a tentative paw reached out. Then a black cat emerged, its ears flattened, its body low to the ground. The other cat refused to leave its carrier. When Mark looked inside, he saw another black cat.

"How can you tell them apart?" he asked.

"The one who came out—Wentworth—has a patch of white on his chest. Darcy doesn't."

"Huh."

He wished he were more of a conversationalist. To his surprise, he wished his older brothers were here. Harrison always knew what to say, while Caleb could make people laugh with his droll one-liners. Even having Jubilee here would be better than this awkward silence, with her incessant chatter and questions. But Mark had never been good at small talk.

Thanks for coming to stay at my place after I bullied you into coming? Yeah, that'll work.

"I'll let you unpack," he said before leaving the room.

WHEN ABBY HAD DRIVEN up and seen Mark standing out in the sun, she'd shivered. Not because she'd been afraid, but because she was...what? Excited? She didn't know how to feel about all of this, if she were honest.

It was such a strange arrangement, something out of a movie. She kept waiting for someone to pop out of the bushes and yell that it was a prank for some reality show.

She took in the house as Mark led her to her room. She truly hadn't expected a house that was so...normal. She'd almost expected turrets and barricades, a true castle for a beastly man.

This house was full of light, the furniture neither gaudy nor overly plain. She couldn't help but notice that there weren't a lot of personal touches, though. Where was Mark in this house? The knickknacks, the photos, the magazines and books?

Mark took her bags inside without saying anything, which gave her a chance to take in his firm backside. He looked very good in those jeans he wore. With that stubble on his jaw and his gruff demeanor, he reminded her of an outlaw from the Wild West.

She desperately wanted to ask him why he'd made her

come here. If not for sex, then what? Companionship? Was he that lonely?

She remembered that kiss yesterday, and her body tingled. Although she'd told him no touching, that declaration had disappeared the moment his lips had touched hers. Had she been the only one to feel the spark between them as their lips brushed, though? She didn't think so.

He'd done it to rile Derek, she told herself. *This is all for show. Don't get sucked into something that isn't real.*

She smiled to see both cats already sitting on the windowsill in her new bedroom.

She stroked Darcy's head. "Do you think you'll be happy here?" she asked them both. Darcy purred while Wentworth butted her hand. "Please don't rip up the toilet paper, or puke a hairball on Mark's bed, or rip up any furniture, okay?"

The cats swished their tails, not making any promises.

She heard footsteps, and turning to see Mark standing in the doorway, she had to bite back a smile at how awkward he looked. She shouldn't find this as amusing as she did. If she were smart, she'd drive home and not look back.

Abby couldn't help but consider this as an adventure. He *was* paying her, and although her nursing job paid the bills, any extra cash was welcome.

"I kind of feel like Belle in *Beauty and the Beast,*" she remarked. "I almost expected the wardrobe to talk to me, or for a candlestick to start dancing."

"I've never seen that movie."

She looked at him in shock. "Seriously? Not even as a kid? That is the saddest thing I've ever heard. It's one of my favorites."

He grunted, looking uncomfortable. "I don't get cartoons.

Anyway, do you need anything else? I need to get back to work."

"Well, I guess, what do you want me to do? You are paying me. I guess you're my boss now."

He rubbed the back of his neck. "Whatever you think is best. I'm not going to give you a list of tasks or anything." Before he left, he added, "And I'll pay you two thousand a week. That all right?"

"That's fine," she replied, a little stunned.

He nodded and left her alone again.

If he were the beast in this scenario, he was doing a terrible job of it. Two thousand a week? He must be crazy.

"Isn't he supposed to lock me up in his dungeon or something?" she asked both cats. "Demand that I stay with him if I want my dying father to go free? Not pay me an exorbitant amount of money to sleep in his guest room?"

Wentworth ignored her and instead threw himself at the window screen when a bug flew past.

Abby decided to explore. Once again, she thought of *Beauty and the Beast*, wondering if there was a west wing she should avoid. She wandered about, touching tables and furniture.

Although it was a pretty house, she had to admit, it was impersonal. It didn't look like anyone lived here. If it weren't for the dishes near the sink or the boots inside the front door, she'd never know anyone lived here.

When she got to Mark's bedroom, she looked over her shoulder to make sure he wasn't behind her. She shouldn't wander into his bedroom, but she also had an insatiable curiosity for mysteries. And at any rate, both cats were playing on Mark's bed, so she could say that she came in here to get them if he caught her snooping.

"Don't rip that up!" She picked up Wentworth from trying to climb a curtain. The cat darted into the adjoining bathroom, and she heard a crash not soon after.

"Out!" She picked up both cats and tossed them out of the bedroom, which earned her flattened ears and a few howls of protest. She shut the door behind her, and then she realized she was now in Mark's room with no real excuse for being there.

You should leave, she told herself. *A bedroom is a private place.*

Listening for footsteps, she decided that she could at least look, right? She wasn't planning on going through his underwear drawer or anything.

His bedroom reflected him, she thought: straightforward, without fuss. He had a large bed built of dark wood, and it was easily the most expensive piece in the room.

Abby couldn't stop herself from wondering what it would be like to be in that bed with him. She flushed, biting the inside of her cheek. Running a hand down the comforter, she smiled at how soft it was. *So he likes nice bedding.* She could appreciate a man who understood the importance of high-thread counts.

The right side table had some books, an empty glass, and a pair of reading glasses. Abby read the titles of the books—all nonfiction about wars or horses—and wandered around the rest of the room.

There was a dresser with a wooden box on it. A tall lamp in the corner. A basket, a bookshelf with a few more titles. It smelled like hay and cedar, but there were no pictures on the walls.

The only photo was on his dresser, the first photo she'd seen in the house. It was of his entire family, including some of the Thornton siblings Abby had yet to meet. The resemblance between all six siblings was rather uncanny, she thought.

Mark stood at the back, Harrison and Caleb beside him. Another Thornton brother—Abby didn't know his name—stood next to Caleb, and then the two sisters sat in front. Dave Thornton stood with his boys while Lisa sat with the girls. Dave had his hand resting on Lisa's shoulder, and although they both looked serious, the photo was a happy one. Abby noted that Mark didn't smile, though. When did that man ever smile?

As she touched the frame, though, something slipped from behind it. It was another photo. Curious, she picked it up. This photo was of a woman. She was beautiful, with dark auburn hair and a bright smile; her smile seemed to be for the photographer. The woman sat in a garden, and she had a rose in her hand.

A bite of envy tugged at Abby's heart. This wasn't a photo of a sister or a family member. Although the woman was fully clothed, the picture was almost sensual in its composition. And the woman gazed at the person behind the camera with love in her eyes.

So why had Mark hidden the photo like this? Had he been the photographer? Had he loved this woman?

"What are you doing?"

Abby yelped and in her haste to place the photo back where it belong, she hit her elbow on the corner of the dresser. She swore.

Mark raised a dark eyebrow.

She tried to find some kind of excuse, and the only one she could come up with was, "The cats were in here."

He looked around. "They're not in here now."

A blush climbed up her cheeks. Rubbing her bruised elbow, she tried to move past Mark, but he stayed her with a light touch.

"What were you doing in here?" he asked again. He didn't sound angry. If Abby didn't know better, he sounded bored. Uninterested. Only his furrowed brows gave away that he was even slightly annoyed.

It was the same voice he'd used when he'd given her his ultimatum. It was a tone that tried to hide how he really felt.

His face darkened when he saw the photo of the woman. Opening the top drawer, he tossed the picture inside and closed the drawer in a quick movement. He leaned against the dresser now, unmoving.

"I'm sorry," she said. "I shouldn't have snooped. I was curious. That photo—"

"Is none of your business." His tone brooked no argument. "I need groceries." He handed her a wad of cash. "Can you go get some?"

"What do you want? Or need?"

"Doesn't matter. Just get food. Isn't that what you're here for?"

She smarted at his tone. She almost opened her mouth to ask more questions, but Mark was already walking away. She followed, feeling foolish and guilty. She'd poked the hornet's nest, hadn't she?

"Wait!" She raced after Mark, following him outside. "Look, I'm sorry. I shouldn't have pried. It's none of my business who that woman was."

"You had no right to look around like that. Can't a man get some damn privacy in his own home?" he rumbled before stalking away.

Abby sighed. Feeling a feline body curl around her ankle, she reached down to pick up Darcy, who'd followed her outside.

"I guess we pissed off the beast, didn't we?" she said, wondering what the hell she'd gotten herself into.

CHAPTER FIVE

Mark worked until his arm ached like the devil. His head hurt, he was thirsty, and he needed to take another Vicodin. He didn't want to—painkillers made him loopy and sick to his stomach—but that was better than the fire burning in his arm.

"You just had to throw me, didn't you?" he asked his horse Samson. Samson snorted and pawed the ground, not the least bit sorry for unseating his rider.

Although Samson was young, he was usually an easy ride, but not when he ran into snakes. Mark hadn't even noticed the snake in their path before Samson had reared. Not expecting it, Mark had landed on his left arm, snapping the bone with a sickening cracking sound.

Mark had been stubborn, not believing he'd broken it. It was a sprain; it would heal on its own. Until the pain had gotten so bad that he'd had to accept that he'd broken it, while Charlie had bullied him to go to the hospital.

Now he not only had a broken arm in a cast and sling, but he had a beautiful nurse running about his ranch. That same nurse he'd been rude to earlier because he was as prickly as a hedgehog. He rubbed his temples as he entered the house, not sure if Abby would speak to him.

He needed to apologize. When he saw that her car was still in the driveway, he had to admit, he'd been surprised. He'd expected her to leave without a goodbye. He'd acted like a total jerk, and over one measly photo.

He inhaled the scent of cooked meat and onions, and his stomach rumbled. Had she really cooked? His gut twisted with guilt. He didn't deserve that.

After cleaning up and changing his clothes, he walked into the kitchen to see Abby cooking away like she'd lived here for years. Like a wife would.

He didn't know what this feeling was in his chest—joy? Terror? She whistled off-key as she cooked, periodically shooing the cats off of the counter. It was a scene he never thought he'd see in his kitchen.

He cleared his throat. Abby looked up, startled.

"Oh, you're back." She wiped her hands on a tea towel, but then she seemed not to know what to do next. "Are you hungry?"

"Yeah. It smells good in here."

She shrugged. "You had no food, so I got as much as I could while in town. I didn't feel like eating microwave dinners. It's just chicken marsala—nothing fancy."

She didn't *sound* upset, but then again, she didn't seem all that happy to see him, either.

"You didn't need to cook for me," he said quietly.

"I didn't. I cooked for myself. There just happens to be enough for us both."

So she was upset. He frowned.

Silence fell. Mark stuffed his hand into his pockets, rocking back on his heels. Staring up at the ceiling, he said, "Look, I'm sorry for what happened earlier. In my bedroom. I was out of line."

When Abby didn't reply, he looked at her face, wondering what she was thinking. She'd moved to lean against the counter, her arms crossed over her chest.

"You were rude," she said bluntly. "I shouldn't have been snooping, but you could've handled it better. You acted like I tried to kill your dog."

He winced.

"Look, when I said I'd help you, I meant it. But I'm not going to stay if you snap at me. I don't care if you tell everyone that we're not dating. I have my pride, too."

He had to respect her for her honesty. Most women would've been in tears, but not Abby. She looked at him straight on, unafraid and unintimidated. He couldn't stop the smile creasing his face.

She didn't reply for a moment. He waited, impatiently, expecting her to say she'd pack her things right then and there.

"You know why I really said yes to this?" she asked.

He shook his head.

"One, because I don't want my mom to know that I lied to her. And two, you're like a puzzle I can't figure out."

"A puzzle?" He didn't know if he should be amused or offended.

"You insult me, snap at me, and then you tell my ex that we're together to get him off of my back." She looked up at him, and her gaze hit him square in the chest. "So, yeah, you're a puzzle."

He struggled with how to explain his motives. Finally, he muttered, "I'm not good with people."

Her lips quirked up. "I figured."

She didn't say anything else, and it drove him insane. What was she thinking? Why was she silent when she hadn't been silent since he'd met her?

She shrugged. "Well, I think I will stay, if it's all the same to you. I needed a change of scenery, you're paying me, and I like mysteries. Let's call a truce."

Smiling a little, he said, "Truce."

"Good. Just FYI, you look like hell. Are you in pain right now?"

He wanted to deny it, but she could see right through him. He nodded.

"Eat something before you take a Vicodin. It'll help with any nausea. I bought some apples. Eat one of those and have a glass of water. You're probably dehydrated as well."

He didn't know whether he should smile or roll his eyes at her tone, but he couldn't deny that he liked that she cared. That she wanted to stay. That he hadn't screwed everything up like he always did.

When he was about to sit down for dinner, he almost didn't see the cat on the chair. It didn't help that the cushions on the kitchen chairs were black, and so the cat was all but invisible. It was only when the cat opened its eyes, golden and sleepy, that he noticed the feline curled in a neat ball.

Abby saw his predicament and laughed. "You can pick him up and move him. He won't bite."

Mark stared at the cat; the cat stared back. Then the cat stretched its paws, extending its claws, and Mark decided he'd sit somewhere else.

"Do you mind if they sit on the furniture? I didn't even think to ask." Abby set down platters of food, and Mark inhaled the amazing aroma. "I'm so used to cats everywhere I forget other people don't like it."

"I don't mind." And he didn't. It was nice to have company, feline included.

"They'll probably try to follow you into the bathroom and your bedroom if you close the door. Cats hate closed doors."

"Why?"

She laughed. "Who knows. Cats are weird. They hate the idea that they're missing out on something. Or that you dared to keep them out."

"Isn't everybody like that?"

She blinked. "I guess so. Nobody likes to get left out, do they?"

Mark grunted, rather wishing he hadn't said anything.

They began eating, not talking much. Abby seemed like she didn't know what to say, while Mark struggled to find something to talk about. He could always talk about his horses, his ranch, his work, but would Abby want to listen to that? He doubted it. Most women would find talk of farm work tedious at best, painful at worst.

"So did you grow up here in Fair Haven?" he asked her after he'd sorted through one question after another, trying to find a suitable one.

She finished swallowing a bite of chicken. "No, I grew up in eastern Washington, near Spokane. I moved here when I got my position at Fair Haven Memorial."

"How long have you been here, then?"

"About five years. You grew up here, right?"

He considered. That was a loaded question. His family

had lived in Fair Haven for decades. The Thorntons were like the royal family of Fair Haven; they were the wealthiest and most influential in the town and general area. Mark had always hated the snobbery of his family, and he'd never lived up to his parents' lofty expectations.

"I was born in Fair Haven like the rest of my siblings. Went to high school there and all that."

"And college?"

He swallowed, the memories rising. College meant Tina. The old pain resurfaced like it always did. He shrugged it off with a grim smile. "College at Western, then I came back to start my ranch. That's about it."

Abby raised an eyebrow. "Really?"

"I don't want to talk about me, though. I'm boring." He sipped his water. "Tell me about you."

ABBY WONDERED WHERE TO START. She thought again about *Beauty and the Beast,* when the Beast had ordered Belle to eat with him and she'd refused. In the fairy tale, she hadn't refused, but instead had gone to dinner with him. At dinner each night, he'd asked her to marry him. And every time, she refused—until one night when she didn't.

Mark, though, wasn't a beast. He was gruff and he wasn't good at small talk. But she had a distinct feeling this was due to shyness.

What was it about him that she found so intriguing? After he'd been rude to her earlier, she should've run back home. She'd known that, and yet she'd gone to buy groceries with the money he'd given her. And then she'd made dinner.

She'd been angry with him as she'd shopped for food. She'd wanted to hit him with something very hard, or at least, demand an apology.

Her anger had faded when she'd seen him in the kitchen, looking so forlorn.

In all honesty, Abby wanted to uncover his mysteries, to unlock whatever was inside this aloof man. It didn't help that he was so attractive, with his chiseled jaw and arresting features, his eyes a deep green.

Was it merely her hormones at play? Was she so easily led astray by a handsome man?

She didn't think so. His good looks aside, she wanted to know *him*. She wanted to understand what was underneath all of those layers and walls.

Now he wanted to know about her. Well, that was better than him growling at her for looking at a photo. She wanted to know about the woman in the photo, but she sensed that would need to wait.

"Let's see, I was born in a place called Tripton. It's a tiny town thirty miles outside of Spokane. I grew up there for the most part, although we lived in Spokane for a few years when I was a teenager. I did my nursing program at Gonzaga, and then got my current job. That's about it."

"What about your parents?"

"My mom lives in Fair Haven now as well. I'm an only child, and my dad died when I was four. So it's been us two for as long as I can remember."

"She never remarried?"

"No, and not because she was so in love with my dad. She just wasn't interested." Abby shrugged. "I think with a daughter to raise and having to work multiple jobs, dating wasn't on the table for her."

Despite her insistence on Abby marrying, Fiona had given up on remarrying for her own sake. She told Abby she was too old now. Any man her age would be a divorcé or a widower, and she didn't have time for that kind of baggage. Men her age wanted younger women anyway. So instead of focusing on her own love life, she focused on Abby's.

"But she wants you to get married." He watched her, his brows furrowed. "Why?"

Abby tried not to blush, mostly out of embarrassment. "She doesn't want me to be alone, I guess. She's kind of old-fashioned. She thinks there's no way I can be happy without a man."

"And can you? Be happy without one?"

Now she raised her eyebrows. "That's quite a question to ask somebody that you don't know, isn't it?"

"I think we're past being acquaintances, aren't we?"

Had they passed that point? There was still so much about Mark she didn't know. She'd only begun to peel back the layers to find who the man was within. Right now, he remained a cipher, the details hazy and his motives even hazier.

"Ever since I broke up with Derek," she said, "my mom has wanted me to start dating again. She was probably more devastated over our breakup than I was."

Mark grunted, his attention now on cutting the chicken on his plate.

"And now, a year after my breakup, I get to hang out with you," Abby said. Her tone was sunny, teasing, and it elicited a small smile from him. "Since I've bored you with the details about myself, I want to know about you. No, you don't get to say no this time. Why did you want to start a ranch?"

He didn't answer right away. Mark seemed like the type of man who preferred to gather his thoughts before speaking. She waited—somewhat impatiently.

"I wanted something completely my own," he said, "not something connected to my family. I wanted to own something that I'd built myself, and I wanted a place that was away from...everything."

"From your family?"

"I guess. My family can be a lot to handle. I didn't want to be under their thumbs. And I've always loved horses."

And he'd started his ranch, most likely without much help, and it had flourished. How many people could say the same?

"This might be a stupid question, but how do you maintain this place?" she asked.

"You mean how do I make any money?" At her nod, he laughed a little. "From lots of things: cattle and dairy farming is one. I also rent acreage to other farmers for grazing. I have an apple orchard, and I recently began to sell goat's milk, but that's a smaller venture. And I've begun breeding horses."

Her eyes lit with curiosity. "Wow. Impressive. And you do it all by yourself?"

"Not exactly. You haven't met Charlie; he does a lot around here. I also have workers that milk the cows, other people that help with harvesting, things like that. But I take care of the horses and do a lot of the work myself."

"Even with a broken arm?"

His smile was wry. "Even with a broken arm."

Abby smiled. "Does your family visit here often?"

He shook his head. "My brothers have a few times, but

they have their own lives. My parents have been here once. My mom..." He shrugged. "She's not much for ranching. She thinks it's beneath me."

Abby had heard enough about Lisa Thornton to know what Mark meant by that statement. She couldn't blame him from wanting to leave Fair Haven with a mother like that.

"I've always wondered what it would be like to have siblings." At his incredulous look, she laughed. "Really. It's lonely being an only child. You have five siblings, right?"

"Yes, and they're a pain in the ass." Despite his words, she could tell he said that with affection. "I'm in the middle: two older brothers, and then two younger sisters and one younger brother."

"What was it like, having that many siblings?"

"Loud." He smiled, remembering. "Crazy. You never had any privacy. Me, Harrison and Caleb were always wrestling and getting into trouble, and then Seth joined us when he was older. The girls got into their own kind of trouble, although Lizzie would wrestle with us and then scream and cry when she lost. She was a brat." He smiled fondly.

Abby's heart did a little twist. She wanted to hear everything about his childhood, his siblings, and his family. She wanted to know why he kept himself apart now. Avoiding his mother was one thing; what about the rest of his family?

"But now everybody has their own lives," he said. He began to gather dishes to take to the sink. "So we aren't as close as we were when we were younger."

"Your oldest brother is engaged, right? To Sara Flannigan?"

"That's right."

He didn't offer any opinions on his brother's upcoming

nuptials. Did Mark want a wife? A family? She almost asked him, but right then, Darcy jumped up onto the counter and began to push at a glass with his paw.

"Darcy! No!"

Mark caught the glass before it fell right as Abby picked up the cat. Darcy meowed in protest.

"Bad cat! Sorry, they love to knock stuff over."

"It's fine. Thanks for making dinner." His eyes darkened a little. "It was good."

Her heart did a little flip flop. "You're welcome."

CHAPTER SIX

After taking a shower and getting dressed for bed, Abby sat in her room and tried to read. Then she tried to watch TV, but she couldn't concentrate on anything. Finally, she tried to go to sleep, but Darcy and Wentworth decided that it was time to run around like demons, almost knocking over a lamp in the process.

She shooed them out when they darted over her head. "I do not need a claw to the eyeball," she groused at them as they sprinted out into the dark hallway. Hearing a thump, she winced, hoping they didn't damage anything during their nightly play sessions.

Leaving the door open a crack so the cats could come back in, she got into bed and stared at the ceiling. She couldn't sleep, though; not with everything she'd learned about Mark whirling in her brain. How did he manage to anger her one moment and pique her curiosity the next?

The self-conscious part of her brain scolded herself, telling her that a man like him would never want her. *Mousy nurse, remember?*

And yet, despite all evidence to the contrary, she didn't believe he'd meant those words. That didn't mean they hadn't hurt, but what had been the motivation to say them at all? A man who thought you were mousy didn't look at you like he wanted every inch of you.

She hugged herself, shivering a little.

Abby sighed, punching a pillow in her frustration with both herself and Mark. She refused to wallow, and she refused to let any stupid man make her feel badly about herself.

So what if she weren't tall, blonde, and skinny? There were too many of those types of women in the world anyway. Why should she be another member of the status quo of supposed female attractiveness?

She started when something thumped against her door. Thinking it was a cat, she got up to open the door wider, only to find that this was no cat.

It was Mark—and he wasn't wearing a shirt.

Good lord.

Her eyes widened, her heart fluttering into her throat. With his defined pectorals, chiseled abdomen, and bulging arms, he was the definition of *yummy.*

It was only when Mark made a noise in his throat that she realized she'd been staring. Was she drooling? *Oh God, I'm an idiot.*

"One of your cats is under my bed," he said, his voice like dark chocolate and velvet wrapped together. "It won't come out."

It took Abby a second to remember that she had a cat. Two cats, to be precise. All she saw was muscles, brown skin, and a man who made her mouth water. *Sexy sexy sexy sexy sexy* her mind chanted.

Mark rubbed the back of his neck. "Uh, Abby?"

She blushed to the roots of her hair. "Oh! Geez, yes!" She hurried past him. She'd been gawking at him like some teenage girl at her first boy band concert. She wanted to hide under the nearest rock and never come out.

When she got to Mark's room, she heard the telltale howl of an unhappy cat. Wentworth paced nearby, his tail twitching.

"Darcy? What are you doing under there?" She crouched down, flipping the comforter up, and she saw yellow eyes blinking at her. "Are you stuck?"

Darcy mewed. It was a very pathetic mew, one she knew well. More than likely, he wasn't stuck; he was upset that he'd ended up in a room without Abby in it. Darcy was a total mama's boy.

She clucked at him. "Come on, Darcy. Let's go to bed. Here, kitty, kitty, kitty. Come on. There you go, let's get out of Mark's room so he can go to sleep."

After some more coaxing, Darcy emerged from under the bed. He meowed at Abby in question. She picked him up, and he started purring immediately.

"Sorry about that," she said.

To her immense disappointment, Mark had put on a shirt. *A damn shame*, she thought with a sigh.

"I let them out of my room to play," she explained. "They probably got lost, being in a new place."

"It's fine."

He didn't say anything else, and so Abby took that as her cue to leave. But she didn't see Wentworth next to her foot. Bumping into the cat, she heard a howl of protest before she started to fall, Darcy tumbling from her arms. Both cats took off from the room like their tails were on fire.

She heard an *oof*, and then a strong arm caught her. A few moments later, she looked up into Mark's dark green gaze, a gaze now filled with a heat that took her breath away.

~

MARK HAD TRIED to get the damn cat out from under his bed himself, but he'd had no luck. So he'd had no choice but to find Abby, which he'd known was a terrible idea the second she'd opened her door, wearing nothing but a tank top and shorts.

Her outfit wasn't sexy in the usual sense: her shorts were rather billowy and her tank wasn't form-fitting, but on her, it was sexy. Her tank showed off the curve of her shoulders while the short shorts showed off her toned legs. He'd almost forgotten what he'd been about to say when she'd opened the door.

Then, to make things worse, she'd had her round ass up in the air as she'd coaxed her cat from under the bed. He'd almost groaned at the sight, telling his unruly cock to calm itself because he was *not going to do this.*

She was his guest. She was a good person.

She had an ass that would make a god weep.

And, now, he held her He'd reacted without thought when he'd seen her about to fall down, catching her in his arms. Now he had a warm bundle of heavenly-smelling female in his arms, and he didn't want to let her go.

Abby's eyes were wide with surprise, a slight flush on her cheeks. Neither of them said anything.

He wanted to say—oh, he didn't know. Everything and nothing.

Mostly, he wanted to kiss her. For a second time. That kiss at the hospital? It hadn't been nearly enough.

A voice in his head whispered that he should leave her alone, that she wasn't the woman for him. But he told that voice to shut the hell up. Leaning down, he waited for her to slap his face, or to tell him to let her go.

Instead, her mouth opened slightly, and that was all the invitation he needed.

When he pressed his mouth to hers, he groaned. Her lips were silky soft, like rose petals, needing her as close as possible. She whimpered and her hands rested on his chest. Could she feel how hard his heart was pounding? Because it was pounding so hard he couldn't catch his breath.

The kiss was almost tentative at first. He felt rusty, unused to kissing, and she seemed shy in her response, like she wasn't sure how he'd react to her. But when he felt her breasts press against his chest, he deepened the kiss without another thought.

Mark wasn't interested in poetry, or love songs, or anything sappy like that. He knew horses and he knew his ranch, and he'd had good sex with pretty women in his lifetime.

But as he kissed Abby Davison, something that had been holding his heart chained began to loosen. He wondered if those poets had been onto something after all.

But poetry reminded him of love and love reminded him of when he'd fallen for a woman who'd betrayed him, and everything came crashing back in an instant.

He stilled; Abby stiffened. She pulled away, giving him a

confused look. When he stepped back and shook his head, he saw hurt flash in her eyes.

"I shouldn't have done that," he said. "I'm sorry."

She breathed hard, a flush now on her chest. The redness deepened with his words, and guilt assailed him. He was a total ass. Hadn't he vowed to leave this woman alone?

Maybe you should've considered that before you brought her to your damn house, he thought irritably.

"You should go," he said.

Abby stiffened her spine and marched out of the room, not saying a word. He winced when he heard her bedroom slam a second later.

CHAPTER SEVEN

Abby had never been so happy to go to work. When the ER bustled with activity, one patient after another coming through its doors, she said a little prayer of thanks. It kept her mind off of other things.

Things like Mark. And Mark kissing her.

She'd barely slept the night before. Tossing and turning, her body hot with both desire and humiliation, she'd dreamed of kicking Mark in the shins. She'd dreamed of kissing him, and then maybe kicking him again for good measure.

She'd tossed and turned so much that the cats had slept on a chair together instead of curled up next to her like they usually did.

By the afternoon, Abby was finally able to sit down. She let out a sigh of relief when Janine handed her a cup of coffee.

"Did you explain to Mrs. Finley that she can't drive while taking her medication?" she asked Janine before taking a long drink of her coffee. "I told her at least three times, but she kept interrupting me."

Janine rolled her eyes. "Yeah, I told her, but I had to tell her husband to make sure she didn't drive. He understood me, at least."

They both drank their coffee in silence, resting their feet until the next round of patients came through the ER doors. Today had been busy, but there hadn't been any cases more complicated than a broken toe or a heart attack scare that had turned out to be a panic attack.

Normally Abby and Janine gossiped when they took their breaks, but Abby's thoughts were back at the ranch.

How could one kiss knock her off of her feet like that? She'd felt it all the way in her bones. She'd felt like she was soaring—and then she'd fallen flat on her face when Mark had told her he hadn't meant to kiss her in the first place.

Save me from idiotic men, she thought. Could they never make up their minds? One second they hated you, then they kissed you. Then they apologized for kissing you.

When Abby had gotten up this morning, she'd considered taking the cats and leaving for good. She had no reason to stay. She didn't care if Mark told everyone about her ruse. The town would enjoy the story and Abby would suffer from the whispers and the talk, but she'd survive. She'd survived much worse.

But something had stopped her from leaving. She told herself it was because she didn't have time to take the cats back to her place before going to work, but that had been a paltry excuse.

"Are you all right?" Janine asked her, breaking her reverie.

Abby almost sloshed coffee onto her hand. Grimacing, she nodded. "I'm fine. Just preoccupied."

"Hmmm. You know, it's funny, a little bird told me some-thing about you that I've been meaning to ask you about."

"What did you hear?"

"I heard that your lovely ex came by to bug you. But then he was sent away with his tail between his legs because, appar-ently, you're dating another guy."

Turning to look her friend in the face, Abby had to bite back a smile at Janine's eager expression. "Who told you that?"

"Doesn't matter. Is it true?" Janine leaned closer, lowering her voice to a whisper. "Are you dating Mark Thornton, aka, the hunkiest rancher ever?"

Abby debated what she should tell her friend. Did she confess that the relationship was completely fake? That it had somehow gotten out of hand and now she was staying with Mark because her life was one bad decision after another?

She sipped her coffee instead.

"You're killing me!" Janine whined. "You have to give me the deets right now, otherwise I'm going to find out from someone else—"

"Fine, fine! But you have to keep it to yourself." Abby whispered the next words: "We aren't really dating, but I am staying at his house."

Janine's eyes widened until they were saucers. "What? Are you serious? Oh my God. So, wait, you aren't together? Now I'm confused."

You're not the only one. "I might have told my mom when she was here that I was dating him, and he overheard me. One thing led to another..."

"Oh my God, is he blackmailing you? Using you for his own illicit purposes?" Janine asked, her tone a mix of horror and excitement. Janine read a lot of thriller novels that tended to bleed into her everyday life.

Abby laughed. "It's not that exciting. He wants me to help around the house in exchange for not telling everyone I lied about us dating."

"That's boring, but also, kind of weird. That's all he wants? He's a Thornton, for Christ's sake! Like he can't hire an actual maid to scrub his floors?" Janine narrowed her eyes, assessing Abby. "There's more to this that you aren't telling me. I can feel it."

Abby wished for an interruption right this moment. But when the universe gave her Derek, she wished she hadn't made a wish at all.

"Oh good, there you are," Derek said cheerfully. "Do you have a second, Abs?"

Why the hell would Derek not leave her alone? Janine, in her usual way, rolled her eyes. She knew all about Derek.

"Janelle, you're looking well," Derek said. He smiled, his teeth gleaming in the bright light of the hospital.

Janine rolled her eyes again. "It's Janine. Abby, we should get back to work."

"You go on; I'll join you in a bit."

When Janine looked like she was going to protest, Abby mouthed *please*. After another glare directed at Derek, Janine took off.

"What is it?" she asked as she stood up. She tossed her coffee in a nearby trash can and waited. *I wish I could toss him into a trash can.*

Derek tried to look abashed. "I'm sorry I keep bothering you like this, but you won't answer my calls or texts. I needed to see you." He lowered his voice. "I've missed you."

She barely restrained herself from rolling her eyes. *I'm plagued with idiotic men, aren't I?*

"Look, I have to get back to work. Can we talk later?"

She tried to step away, but he caught her by the elbow. "I know, I screwed up. I get it. But I should never have let you go. It's something I've regretted every day since we broke up."

He maneuvered them both so they were in an alcove, away from prying eyes and ears. "I want you back, Abby. Tell me it's not too late."

She was completely at a loss. If he'd missed her so much, why tell her a year later? The old Abby would believe in his sincerity, but the more realistic Abby knew that this wasn't because he loved her. Or at least not the type of love she wanted anything to do with.

"I already told you that we're over. When I said that a year ago, I meant it. We aren't good for each other. You know that as well as I do."

Derek's lips thinned, and Abby saw the sharper edges of the man she'd once thought she loved. "Because you're with him now? Mark Thornton?"

Hearing him say Mark's name sent a frisson of heat down her body, although it combined with an almost painful longing. "Yes, we're together," she said. "So whatever it is you think you need to say? Don't."

She moved to leave, but he caught her arm. His grip tightened. When she looked at his expression, she almost shivered.

"He'll never love you like I do. He's a Thornton. They only love their own. Do you think his family will let him be with a woman like you?" His voice turned into a whisper, but it still wrapped around her heart like barbed wire. "A woman who can't even be a real woman for him?"

Her blood turned to ice. Gasping for breath, she wrenched her arm from him. She felt tears building, but she forced them away. She would not cry in front of this asshole.

"Mark doesn't care about that. And anyway, it's none of your business." She drew herself up, her chin lifted. "I'm going back to work. Don't bother me again or I'll call security."

She didn't wait to hear Derek's reply. When she found Janine minutes later, she was grateful her friend didn't ask her why her eyes were red.

MARK STARED at the two cats who sat in his living room window, their tails swishing in unison. He hadn't expected to see them this morning, if he were honest. He'd expected to see the cats—and Abby—long gone.

One of the cats turned and gave him the evil eye, his whiskers twitching. Mark frowned.

Why the hell hadn't she left?

It was that thought that trailed him as he worked through the morning and afternoon. It was total deja vu from the day prior. Mark insulting Abby, Mark expecting her to leave, Abby staying. He asked Delilah about it, but she only snorted and demanded another nose rub.

He seemed to be in a perpetual cycle of insulting Abby and then apologizing to her. Would he never learn not to insult her in the first place? He winced as he carried hay bales into the barn. Sweat dripped from his brow, and his arm ached. The day he got this damn cast off he'd throw the stupid thing into the fire with total glee.

Mark fed the goats, who hopped around him and then

tried to munch on his pant leg. One of the kids jumped onto his back when he bent down, which was how Charlie found him.

"You got something on ya," Charlie said, laughter in his voice.

Mark rolled his eyes. He reached back to get the kid, not wanting to dump it onto the ground, but the kid jumped off of him and scampered away. Mark winced, feeling the bruise forming from those sharp hooves that had dug into his back.

Charlie didn't say anything else for a while as he helped Mark. Mark was thankful that his ranch hand wasn't chatty. He didn't want to talk about his guest, or the fact that he couldn't stop thinking about kissing her.

That kiss had rocked his world. He hadn't known a kiss could do that; it had been like getting tossed into a whirlwind.

"So I guess your lady isn't here?" Charlie asked as the two of them mucked out the horses' stalls. "I thought she was supposed to be here by now?"

Mark grunted. Raking hay took twice as long with one hand, and he grew more aggravated with each passing moment. "She was here. She had to go to work."

"Huh."

Mark knew Charlie wanted to say something. If Charlie had an opinion, he'd tell Mark eventually.

"Well, I keep wondering what the hell would possess you to ask a lady to come all the way out here just to do your laundry."

"She's not doing my laundry," Mark groused.

"Whatever it is you're having her do. Now, looking at you this morning, you look like you didn't get any sleep. I know your arm's been aching, but I know you. I know when you have something on your mind, and I'd bet my last dollar that it has something to do with this woman."

Mark glared at Charlie. Wiping his forehead, he set his hay fork aside. "I'm starving. Want anything?"

"I wonder if you know what you're doing at all."

Mark felt the hairs on the back of his neck stand on end. If he were honest, he'd admit that he'd wondered the same thing so many times it was like an endless loop in his brain.

Charlie's face creased, his gray-streaked brows furrowed. "If you like this lady, then don't screw it all up."

"Because that's what I always do?"

Charlie shrugged. "We all do. We're just bumbling fools around women. Me included. But if she's causing you this much grief? Well, there must be a reason for it, I reckon."

Mark felt Delilah nuzzle his shoulder, and he patted her absently.

Hearing Charlie's words made him realize that he needed to let Abby go, even though the thought twisted his gut. He needed to tell her she could leave whenever she wanted without fear that he'd tell everyone about her lie. It wasn't enough that *he* knew he wouldn't say a word. Abby didn't know that.

His stomach sank to his toes when he realized that she'd leave as soon as she could, but it was the right thing to do.

Mark stroked Delilah's nose, feeling her hot breath against his neck. "She's totally screwing me up," he admitted.

Charlie nodded. "She's a woman. Of course she is."

ABBY RETURNED to the ranch that evening without knowing

why she'd come back. Then again, she needed to collect her things and her cats if she were going to leave. That was what she told herself, at any rate.

She heard voices coming from the barn, and then a man she hadn't met emerged. He was older than Mark, grizzled and tanned, like a man who'd worked his entire life outside. He tipped his hat to her, which made her smile.

"You must be the lady Mark's told me about," he said as he extended his hand. "Charlie Leighton."

"Abby Davison," she replied as she shook Charlie's hand. "Do you work here as well?"

"I help around, yeah. Keep Mark out of trouble, too." He winked.

Right then, Mark came out of the barn, shaking his head. "If anyone's keeping anybody out of trouble, it's me keeping this guy out of trouble." His gaze collided with Abby's, and she caught her breath.

They stared at each other for a long moment until the sound of a horse neighing broke the moment.

Charlie assessed them both. "Well, it's probably high time I got out of here." He smiled at Abby, his look wry. "You keep this guy out of trouble while I'm gone, you hear?"

"Of course. Nice to meet you, Charlie."

Once Charlie drove off, it was the two of them, alone again. Mark stuffed his hands into his pockets while Abby wondered what she should say. Or could say. She waited for him to apologize, or to tell her to get off his ranch for good.

Mostly she wished he'd kiss her again.

Stupid. You don't need that kind of drama in your life.

When a horse neighed again, Mark looked over his

shoulder into the barn. "Let me introduce you," he said suddenly. He walked into the barn before she could respond.

She followed him, curious. She inhaled the scent of hay and horses, sweet and pungent. She counted three horses, one of which was nosing at Mark's shoulder. She was a beautiful chestnut, and as Abby got closer, she saw that the horse was very pregnant.

"When is she due?" she asked. She'd never been around horses, so she kept her distance.

Mark smiled as he stroked the horse's muzzle. "In about a month. This is Delilah." He then pointed at a black horse, "That's Samson," and then he pointed to a gray horse, "And that's Rosemary."

Abby came closer to the pretty chestnut. "Delilah, what a lovely girl," she cooed.

"Let her smell your hand. There you go."

Abby reached her hand toward Delilah, and when the horse mouthed at her fingers, she laughed. Delilah snorted and tossed her head.

"She likes to be scratched right here. Yeah, that's the spot, isn't it?" Mark rubbed her, and her eyes closed in happiness.

Abby petted her, surprised at how soft she was. "I've never ridden a horse," she admitted.

"Never? Well, I'll have to teach you. Nothing as nice as riding a horse on your land."

Watching Mark now, his face softened as he patted Delilah, Abby realized this was a side of Mark few people saw. The Mark that the world tended to see was a guy who was gruff and aloof. But if he were capable of caring for animals like this, it meant he possessed hidden depths.

Her heart squeezed. She had to look away, concentrating instead on Delilah's dark eyes.

"Here," Mark said as he handed her a carrot. "She loves carrots. Keep your hand flat so she doesn't accidentally bite your fingers."

Abby obeyed, and Delilah began to munch on the carrot before taking it completely into her mouth. Abby laughed again.

Mark had her come inside Delilah's stall as he brushed her down. Abby watched him work, his hands gentle, especially as he brushed over the mare's swollen sides.

Abby let out a surprised sound when she saw Delilah's belly ripple. "Oh, you can see the foal!" She moved closer. "Is that a hoof?"

Mark grinned. "Probably. Can't imagine it's too comfortable to have four hooves kicking at you from the inside like that."

"Probably no more comfortable than a human baby kicking you."

At the mention of babies, Abby felt her throat close. Derek's words from earlier in the day came back to her, clawing at her. *He'd want a real woman, wouldn't he?*

And she couldn't be that woman, no matter how much she wanted to be.

"I should get dinner started," she said.

"Wait, Abby."

Her back to him, she waited. He let out a deep sigh.

"I feel like this is all I do lately, but I'm sorry. For last night. I shouldn't have done what I did. Or said."

Abby couldn't move. She hadn't wanted his apology—not

for kissing her. What did it say about a man that he *regretted* kissing you? It meant that he hadn't wanted you.

He'd done it because—she didn't know. He was lonely? She was available? Any other woman would've worked in that instance. She was replaceable, unremarkable.

Anger curdled in her gut. Turning, she said in a tight voice, "I don't know why I keep coming back here."

He looked like he wasn't sure, either. Abby wanted to laugh.

What a mess this is.

She moved toward him until she could see the sheen of sweat on his brow, how his hair curled from his work. How his shirt hugged his torso.

"I don't know what's up with you, or what you think of me, but the last thing I need is some guy kissing me because I'm convenient. So save your apology. I don't want to hear it."

His jaw clenched, his chest rising and falling with heavy breaths. "Is that what you really think?"

"That you kissed me out of pity? What else am I supposed to think?" She crossed her arms over her breasts. "I'm tired of men treating me like I'm disposable. I'm not doing this again."

She waited for him to respond, to say that he was sorry. She waited for him to say, *it's not like that, I wanted to kiss you and only you.* But he said nothing.

She turned away in disgust. Stalking out of the barn, she headed toward the house, but Mark caught her before she got inside.

"Let's get one thing straight," he said, almost growling. The sound sent a shiver down her spine. "You can think whatever you like about me and God knows most of it is probably true, but I did not kiss you out of *pity*." He spat the word with such heat that she gaped at him.

His hand was still on her arm, holding her, and the heat of his fingers on her skin sent desire roaring through her. She wished she weren't so weak for this man.

His eyes darkened, and when he looked like he was going to kiss her, her stupid, traitorous heart thrilled.

But in the last moment, she found the strength to pull away. "I can't keep doing this. This back and forth. Just... no. I'm not doing this."

Mark looked hurt for a second, but he shuttered the expression. Then: "You can go, you know. If you want."

Now she wanted to roll her eyes. Could this man never make up his mind?

"And then you can tell everybody that I'm a lying liar who lies?"

That made his lips twitch. "No. I wouldn't—" He pushed his fingers through his hair. "I wouldn't say anything. I shouldn't have said that I would in the first place. It was low of me. You can add that to the list of things I should apologize for."

She was stunned. Then again, hadn't she sensed that Mark didn't have a malicious bone in his body? He might act rashly when angry or desperate, but he wasn't the type to hold something over a person.

Her anger deflated, and confusion filled her instead. This man would drive her insane if she let him.

"Thank you," she said softly, "I appreciate that. I'll stay one more night and be gone in the morning. That work?"

He looked away, effectively dismissing her. "That's fine."

CHAPTER EIGHT

Abby folded the last of her clothes, shooing away the cats when they tried to climb inside her suitcase. She'd have to leave early in the morning if she wanted to make it to work on time after dropping off the cats.

"You two make my life more complicated, you know that, right?" she said fondly before giving each cat a good scratch. Wentworth meowed and stretched while Darcy yawned and rolled over onto his back.

She sat on the bed and stroked both cats, her thoughts still in turmoil. She needed to leave because she was very much afraid that if she stayed any longer, Mark Thornton would break her heart. Even if he hadn't kissed her out of pity, she had to protect herself.

She sighed as she ruffled Darcy's fur.

"What am I doing?" she whispered. "I've never felt this lost before."

Even when she'd made the decision to break up with Derek she hadn't been this torn up. She felt like one part of her was tugging her to stay, to uncover more of Mark, to discover the vulnerable center of a man who was so closed off. The other part of her told her to run as fast as she could and never look back.

Darcy rubbed his face against her hand. She smiled.

"You guys don't care, do you? No, you don't. Just as long as somebody's there to feed you and scratch you."

The cats yawned and fell back asleep.

Her phone rang, and she grimaced when she saw that her mom, Fiona, was texting her. At least her mother wasn't calling her—she couldn't deal with a phone call right now.

How are you? I haven't seen you in forever! her message read.

Considering she'd seen her mother a few days ago—had it only been a few days since this whole thing had begun?—she couldn't help but smile. Her heart tightened, thinking of her mother.

She was tempted to call her and pour her heart out to her, asking her for her advice like she'd done when Abby had been a kid. What would she tell Abby? Drop him and run, probably.

She hesitated, considering. But then she remembered the look of joy on Fiona's face when Abby had told her she was dating again. Could she disappoint Fiona?

Not yet, she reasoned. She'd let Fiona enjoy the idea of Abby dating a guy like Mark for a little while longer.

Or you don't want to admit that you were never dating the guy to begin with.

Yes, that could be the reason, too.

She replied, *Didn't we just see each other? :)*

Doesn't matter. I was going to call you but I've been busy, too. How's your guy?

Abby tried to find something between the truth and a lie. *He's good. Arm's getting better every day. I try to help with what I can.*

Help? Is that what you're calling it? ;) Well, I'll let you go. Have a good time. Love you.

Love you too, Abby messaged, her gut twisting with guilt. She didn't even want to think about how she'd tell her mother that she and Mark were over. Or that they had never been dating to begin with, although there had been those kisses…

"Ugh!" she exclaimed as she threw a pillow against the wall. Wentworth opened one eye to glare at her; Darcy didn't even move.

As she got ready for bed, she realized that she couldn't find her car keys. They were usually in her purse, but after getting out her lip balm and not hearing the tell-tale jingle of her keys, she dug around, only to come up empty-handed. She huffed out an annoyed breath. Of course she would lose her keys the night before she tried to leave this stupid ranch!

This was the second time she'd lost something around Mark Thornton. Maybe he was like a magnet for important items.

She'd had her keys in her hand when she'd gotten out of her car today... and when she'd been in the barn with Mark. She must've dropped them in there.

Heading outside, she shivered at the cool night air. It was completely dark now, and she stood for a moment looking up at the stars. She hadn't seen the stars this well in ages, not since she'd been camping as a little girl. Gazing up at the faraway constellations, she felt lonely, like she was the last person left on earth. It was her and the stars and nobody else.

Abby shook off the feeling and continued toward the

barn. Right when she was about to enter, she heard a voice. She stilled, waiting.

It was Mark. Why was he out here in the cold? She listened, hoping he was about to leave so she could find her keys.

Then she waited for an entirely different reason as she heard him talking to one of the horses.

"I never say the right thing around her," he said in a low voice. He sounded... pained, almost. "It's like all I ever end up doing is insult her."

Abby held her breath. She knew she should leave him alone, but she was too curious to go back into the house.

The horse made a snuffling sound, and Mark laughed a little. "You think I should get my head out of my ass? Yeah, you're probably right. I keep thinking I should let her be and yet..."

Abby waited on tenterhooks for his next sentence, but there was only silence. She barely stopped herself from letting out an annoyed sound. The man couldn't even let her eavesdrop properly!

She heard movement, and then the sound of patting. "At least I have you, right? You're my forever girl, aren't you, Delilah?" A pause. Then: "You'd never betray me. Not you."

Abby's heart constricted until she felt like she couldn't breathe. She shouldn't be here. Hurrying back to the house, she didn't know what to think except that she'd discovered something about Mark that had not been for her ears.

She thought about the photo in Mark's bedroom. Was that the woman who'd betrayed him? She didn't know if she were angrier with the unnamed woman or more sympathetic toward Mark.

Derek hadn't cheated on her, but he'd never appreciated her, either. Emotionally, he'd never been faithful. It seemed a paltry comparison, but at the same time, she felt a sort of kinship with Mark.

She sneaked into her bedroom and closed the door until it was only slightly ajar so the cats could get out. The two felines looked up at her when she entered, but neither moved from their spots on the bed.

And on her bed was her suitcase, packed and ready to go. She let out a breath she hadn't even known she'd been holding. *I don't want to leave*, she thought. *How can I leave him?*

She didn't know how it had happened, but they'd forged a connection already. She didn't know if it was lust or something deeper, but she couldn't deny that the connection existed.

Yes, he frustrated her and he seemed incapable of keeping his foot out of his mouth. But what if she didn't run away when things got difficult? If she saw this through?

She covered her mouth when a laugh almost burst through. *See what through?* she thought wildly. *This fake relationship that has been nothing but confusing from the beginning?*

When she woke up the following morning, she waited to hear Mark's footsteps. He usually got up with the dawn, and right on cue, she heard his boots against the wooden floor.

She got out of bed before she lost her nerve. Putting on her robe, she followed after him.

"Mark."

He turned, his eyebrows raised in surprise. "Abby?"

She tried not to think about how her hair was probably a rat's nest, or that Mark looked at her like she'd lost her mind.

She realized then that she didn't know how to explain why she wanted to stay when she'd already told him she was leaving. She couldn't very well say, *I heard you talking to your horse last night, hope you don't mind.*

He cleared his throat. "I should get to work, unless you need help packing?"

"No, I don't want your help. Not with packing—because I'm not leaving."

He stared at her.

Feeling a blush climbing up her face, she scrambled for a reason. "I'm not leaving because you still need to show me how to ride a horse. So I'm holding you to that promise. Got it?"

The poor man looked like a tractor had run over him.

"What?"

"You heard me. I have to get to work, but I'll see you later."

She barely bit back a smile as she bustled past him into the kitchen.

MARK GLANCED over his shoulder at Abby. She rode Rosemary at a sedate pace while he rode Samson. Despite her initial trepidation, Abby had embraced horseback riding. In fact, she looked like she was enjoying herself.

Rosemary was an easy ride and didn't mind novices. Unlike Samson, who had the attention span of a gnat, Rosemary tended to plod along on one path and never detour. Mark kept an eye out for snakes, holding Samson's reins more tightly than usual.

He still couldn't believe Abby had stayed, and because she'd wanted to learn horseback riding. What kind of a reason was that? Maybe he'd finally driven her to the brink of insanity.

But she didn't look insane as she leaned over to pet Rosemary's mane. And he didn't imagine the way her eyes gleamed whenever they made eye contact.

He looked off into the horizon. Was she here because she wanted to stay with *him?* It seemed too good to be true. And yet, what other explanation could there be?

His chest clenched, and he squeezed Samson's flanks hard enough that the horse danced in surprise. He soothed the gelding, forcing himself not to transfer his anxiety to the animal. He didn't need Samson throwing him a second time.

Mark focused on the landscape instead. The leaves were all brilliant reds, oranges, and yellows, and the smell of autumn filled the air. He inhaled, finding that the scent centered him. Leaves crunched under the horses' hooves with each step. Before long, the trees would shed their leaves entirely, and they would enter the rainy season.

And by then, Abby would be long gone.

Abby rode up next to him. She was a fast learner, he had to give her that. They didn't say anything as they rode their horses further westward, going along one of Mark's favorite trails. This path could get rather steep, but it was also wide enough that he knew Rosemary could traverse it without difficulty.

"It's beautiful out here," Abby said as she looked at the trees and foliage. "You're lucky to have this."

"I know," was all he said, because he knew it was true. This ranch was everything to him. It had provided a safe haven when the world had seemed to abandon him.

"I thought I'd take you to one of my favorite sights," he said. "It's only about a half mile more this way."

"And then you'll finally toss me off a cliff and be done with me?"

He swiveled toward her, only to see her smiling. He let out a breath.

"I was teasing," she said with a laugh. "Do people never tease you?"

"Only my brothers, if they're being stupid."

That made her smile widen, and she laughed.

But her words lightened his heart. When was the last time a beautiful woman had teased him? Too long.

And Abby was beautiful, especially today. Sunshine glittered in her hair, creating molten streaks of gold within her hair's earthy brown. Freckles had come forth on her face, and she looked rosy. The peak of health. And she also wore the tightest pair of jeans he'd ever seen, which didn't help him with his self-control.

They didn't say anything else until they reached the spot, which overlooked a huge gorge, now covered in trees sporting autumnal leaves. It was all gold and ruby, so gorgeous that it never failed to take his breath away.

"Wow," Abby breathed. "No wonder you love this."

He dismounted before helping her down, leading the horses to graze under a nearby tree. Dismounting with one hand proved tricky, but he managed to avoid falling on his face, thank God. He then pulled out a blanket from his saddlebag and unfolded it.

"You planned this," she said in surprise. "Did you bring a picnic basket, too?"

His lips twitched. "No, but only because it wouldn't fit inside my saddlebag."

She laughed again and sat down next to him. About a foot of space kept them apart, but Mark took that opportunity to study her. To look at the woman who'd agreed to stay with him, even when she knew she could leave. This woman who had endured his foot-in-mouth syndrome with the utmost grace.

"Can I tell you something?" she asked.

He nodded, nonplussed.

"I still don't understand you at all." Her words weren't harsh but curious.

He almost laughed. He didn't understand himself most days. "What do you want to know?"

"Well, I can't figure out if you hate me or not." At his look, she bit back a smile. "Oh come on, you know what I mean. One second you're saying I'm a mousy nurse, the next you're telling me I have to stay with you. Either you're a sadist or there's something else going on here."

He clenched his fingers in the blanket. Her mood seemed playful, but he could feel the barbs under her words, too.

"If you think there isn't anything going on here," he said in a gruff voice, "then you're not as observant as I thought."

That got a reaction: her cheeks turned red, and she looked away. He waited for her to say something else, and he realized with a grimace that he was going to have to be the one to speak first.

"I'm sorry for what I said that day in The Rise and Shine. About you being—well, you know. I didn't mean it."

She raised an eyebrow. "Really? Then why say it at all?"

He rubbed the back of his neck. "Because my brothers

were messing with me, and I wanted them to stop. I didn't expect you to hear what I said."

"That seems to be a running theme for my life lately."

He huffed out a laugh. "It was a shitty thing to do, and I'm sorry." Catching her gaze again, he murmured, "You're not mousy, Abby. You're—everything."

The blush of before increased, but this time, he knew it was from pleasure. Smiling, she plucked at a stray thread on the blanket, suddenly shy.

"I'm sorry, too. For how I responded. I shouldn't have called you an ass."

"I was one, though."

She wrinkled her nose. "True. You were."

He growled, and when she let out a peal of laughter, he didn't think about what he did next. He pulled her close with his good arm, and when she pressed against him, he felt the earth tilt on its axis. She was a warm bundle of curves, all womanly and soft. He cupped her cheek.

Then he kissed her.

He didn't care that he'd told her he'd leave her alone, or that this relationship of theirs was nothing but a sham. The taste of her, the sound of her moan? Those were all real. And his cock pulsing with need was all too real as well.

He licked at her mouth, murmuring at her to open, and she did, letting their tongues touch. He explored her, and she did the same, sending his pulse into overdrive. He couldn't breathe. He couldn't think, either. He could only feel Abby and how she clutched at his shirt.

But then she pulled away and looked up at him with a wide-eyed gaze. "What are we doing?" she breathed.

He shook his head. "Does it matter?"

He waited for her response. Her mind seemed to be working out some conundrum, the wheels turning. Finally, she shook her head.

"No, it doesn't. Just don't stop kissing me."

ABBY WAS afraid her heart would burst from her chest right then and there. When Mark laid her down on the blanket, his body shielding her from the outside world, she arched under him. She needed him to touch her everywhere. She was about to come out of her skin for wanting him.

But then he swore under his breath, making her eyes widen.

He looked at his broken arm apologetically as he sat up again. "I forgot about this," he said.

She smiled and before he could react, she climbed into his lap, hooking her arms around his neck.

"How about this?" she whispered, their noses brushing.

"Perfect."

His breath was hot, and she was close enough that she could see how his lashes curled, dark and dusky. She kissed him, and he groaned her name.

He tasted like the coffee he'd drunk earlier, and his stubble scraped against her chin with each movement of their mouths. Her skin prickled. She wished she could get out of her clothes, because they felt too tight. Too constraining.

Mark's hand smoothed down her back until he reached the hem of her shirt. Shyness filled her, and she wished she'd worn sexier underwear. She wished she were skinner, and tanner, and everything she was not. He seemed to sense her wariness because he stroked her back in soothing motions.

As he traced lazy circles on her spine, she opened her eyes to see him looking at her.

"I love your eyes," she said, because it was true. She'd thought they were like the darkest of forests, a deep evergreen, and she was right. She'd never seen eyes that color.

His lips quirked upward. "They're just green."

She wanted to explain that they weren't just green, but words failed her. Instead, she danced her fingers along his brow and down his cheeks, then along his upper lip. She'd never touched a man like this—not even Derek. This somehow felt unbearably intimate in comparison.

He kissed her fingertips, making her smile. When he tugged at her shirt, she didn't let self-consciousness take over again. She stripped out of her shirt and watched for his reaction. If he were disappointed, it would tell her what she needed to know.

But his reaction wasn't disappointment: it was all fire. His eyes shone, his pupils expanded, and he drank her in for so long that she could feel a flush blooming on her chest.

He used his one hand to pull down one bra strap, then the other. Her heart pounded. When he moved to the clasp next to her sternum, though, she brushed his hand away with a coy smile.

That made him laugh. "I would've figured it out," he said.

"But I'm not feeling that patient."

After letting her bra drop to the ground, she found herself unable to look him in the eye. Her nipples tightened, though, and she couldn't seem to catch her breath.

He touched her breast finally, his fingers glancing over her nipple.

"Come closer," he said.

She moved further into his lap, and she couldn't stop herself from gasping when she felt his hardness press against her. When she wiggled a little, he grunted and forced her to stay still.

He touched and kissed her with a gentleness that made her want to both cry and demand that he go faster, harder. She wanted to dig her nails into his shoulders, shout his name to the sky. She wanted him to mark her and to claim her, make her forget her own name.

But Mark touched her like she was a treasure, and her heart twisted into knots when he kissed her right over that fluttering organ.

He moved her arm so he could lick her nipple, his hand playing with her other breast. Her body burst into flames from those touches.

When she arched and begged and moaned for him to make this ache inside her end, he kissed her mouth, hushing her cries. She wrapped her arms around him like a vine.

"What do you need, Abby?" he breathed against her mouth. "Where do you want me to touch you?"

She'd never had a man ask that, and his focus on her once again made her heart burst with sheer emotion. How had she already fallen for this man? This brusque, mysterious rancher? But despite his rough exterior, she knew he was a man worth knowing.

And perhaps, a man even worth loving.

Her breath caught. Anxiety fluttered inside her, and she pushed away the thought. *I can't fall in love with him. I can't.*

"Abby," he said again. "Abby, Abby, Abby."

She moved off of his lap and, as he watched, she unbuttoned her jeans. His eyes narrowed, a slight flush reddening his cheeks.

She couldn't say the words, but she could show him. Climbing into his lap again, she took his hand and placed it where heat had pooled and where she ached for him.

His nostrils flared. Without another word, he kissed her and pushed his fingers inside her panties, cupping her sex with his palm.

Abby held onto him as he parted her, dipping and petting, his touches once again too light. She tried to rub against him, but he laughed.

"Where do you want me to touch you?" His voice rumbled through her body.

Trembling, she tried to find the words. It was like her brain had floated away from her body, and she was only sensation.

"Higher." She closed her eyes. Her breath hitched when his fingers moved upward. "Yes, God, yes. Right there."

"Someday I'm going to look at you here, all pink and wet and desperate for me. How this little nub" —and he rubbed her on that spot right then, which made her gasp— "grows more swollen as I part your folds. As I lick you, from here to here." He moved his index finger from her clit to swirl around her entrance.

Abby bit her lip. The pleasure was too great. She was going to die, and she wouldn't even care. When Mark began to rub her clit, pushing a finger inside her, she moaned until she was sure the entire forest could hear her.

He kissed her throat, then nipped at her. Sucking the skin

near her shoulder, he rubbed her with relentless strokes as she gasped. Higher, higher, higher, she climbed and climbed and then—she fell.

Shaking and moaning, she felt Mark's arm go around her waist, and he held her close. He kissed her again. Her mind was hazy with lust and fulfillment, her heart bursting from her rib cage.

Abby didn't know what time it was when she finally came back to herself. They were lying on the blanket, Mark watching her with a hooded gaze. She didn't care that she was topless or that her hair was a snarled mess. Moving closer until their bodies pressed against each other, Abby gave him a sweet kiss.

His eyes softened. Stroking her hair, he seemed like he wanted to say something, but then she saw the minuscule shake of his head.

"We should get back," he said finally.

Back to what? she couldn't help but wonder.

CHAPTER NINE

"Abby! Oh my God, how are you?" Megan Flannigan said, rushing to greet Abby. On her lunch break, Abby had driven over to have a quick chat with her good friend at her bakery, The Rise and Shine.

Abby returned the embrace. "I'm good. How about you? How's this place doing?"

Megan waved away her question. "There's no way we're talking about my bakery when you need to tell me *everything*. Yes, everything." Megan looked over her shoulder and said, "Jubilee, will you take over for a bit? I'll be in the back with Abby."

Jubilee gave her boss a thumbs-up before helping the next customer.

Megan had texted Abby on Sunday night, demanding that Abby tell her all the details about her relationship with Mark.

Abby couldn't help but notice how happy Megan looked, her eyes shining. After a tumultuous few years, Megan and Caleb Thornton had finally admitted how much they loved each other. Abby envied her the assurance that Caleb adored her as much as she adored him.

Once they got to Megan's office and shut the door, Megan was bursting with excitement.

"Okay, now you have to give me all of the details. When I heard from Sara that you were dating Mark Thornton, I just about lost my mind."

Sara was Megan's older sister, and the two siblings told each other everything.

Abby tried not to blush, only because she couldn't help but think about how Mark had kissed her yesterday afternoon, and how she'd cried out his name, and how she'd dreamt of him touching her again that night...

"Where did Sara hear it from?" Abby asked instead.

"Somebody from her school mentioned it." Megan smiled. "You know how the grapevine is around here. Nobody can keep a secret. But that doesn't matter, because now you're *living* with Mark? How did that happen?"

Abby debated whether she should confess all, but the weight of her secret was too much to continue to bear alone. She sighed and said, "We aren't really dating."

Megan blinked. "What?"

Abby explained everything: lying to her mom, Mark overhearing Abby and giving her an ultimatum, and moving to his ranch until his arm healed. Megan's eyes got wider and wider as the story progressed. Abby skipped over the kissing, though. She wasn't about to give Megan that level of detail.

But Megan was astute, and she narrowed her eyes at Abby when she finished. "You like him, don't you?"

Abby wanted to deny it. She wanted to shake her head

and laugh at the suggestion, but she couldn't. All she could do was bury her face in her hands and moan.

Megan patted her on the shoulder. "Yes, that's generally every woman's reaction when they start to fall for a Thornton brother. You're not alone."

"What am I going to do?"

"Well, do you have any idea how he feels?"

Abby shook her head, then nodded, then sighed again. "I mean, he's interested in me—you know what I mean. But sometimes I can't tell what's real and what's not, you know? This whole thing started as a sham. Now I'm wondering if any of it is real."

"You know what I think?"

Abby couldn't stop herself from smiling at Megan's lofty tone. "What?"

"I think Mark made that deal with you because he's lonely and he didn't know how else to talk to you." Megan wrinkled her nose. "Talk about a fucked-up, roundabout way of asking a woman out. What is it with these Thornton men?" She said the last sentence with a mix of exasperation and deep fondness.

"I think you're right. He told me I could leave anytime without being afraid that he'd say anything. But I didn't want to leave. How is that for fucked up?"

"Very." Megan smiled. "But I can't judge. Caleb and I were the definition of a screwed-up relationship."

Reaching for Abby's hands, Megan squeezed them. "Just a word of warning: be very sure you know what you're getting yourself into. If Caleb drives me nuts, then Mark is a whole 'nother level, from what I understand. That man has secrets. He's basically shut himself off from the world."

Abby squeezed Megan's hands back. "He does. But so do I. And who am I to judge anyone for having secrets?"

"Well said." Megan rose and opened her office door. "Now let's get some coffee and some pie before you leave, because you definitely need both to deal with this mess."

MARK STARED at the bags of feed, feeling like his brain and his body wouldn't connect. Or maybe it was that his brain was so fixated on how Abby arched her neck as she came. Or how he told himself he should leave her alone, yet that voice inside his head kept shrinking and shrinking with every passing hour.

When somebody brushed past him to get a bag of feed, he jolted back into reality. Mark got what he needed, paid, and headed out.

Right before he got to his truck, he saw the two people he never expected to see again: Tina Gage and Aaron Klein. His ex-girlfriend and his ex-best friend, respectively.

Then again, seeing the wedding rings on their fingers, she'd be Tina Klein now, wouldn't she?

Tina let out a surprised gasp, her hand instinctively going to her protruding belly. Mark swallowed the bile that had risen in his throat, seeing these two together.

He'd thought they'd moved away from Fair Haven long ago, but they still had family here, he supposed. And as fate would have it, he'd run into them on the one day he came to town.

He shifted the bag of feed against his shoulder, refusing to acknowledge them. He wasn't interested in having some polite chat with these two cheaters. He would've let Tina go had she told him that she'd fallen in love with Aaron. It would've hurt, but he wasn't heartless, either.

But the night he'd found them together in his and Tina's bed? A bitter, all-consuming rage had filled him, so much so that he barely remembered that night. He remembered punching Aaron, and Tina screaming, and all three of them running outside. He remembered the tears coursing down Tina's face as she kept saying how sorry she was.

"Mark!"

Mark dumped the bag of feed into the back of his truck before turning around. Tina, damn her to hell, was still as beautiful as he remembered, with her dark auburn hair and dewy skin. She had that pregnancy glow, or whatever it was people said women had when they were going to have a baby. He watched as Aaron put an arm around her, like he needed to protect her from Mark.

Aaron was blond and of average-height, but he'd had a charisma that had charmed both men and women alike. Aaron could get anyone to do what he wanted, whereas Mark had always been stand-offish and awkward.

He and Mark had grown up together and had been room-mates in college at Western. They'd even discussed starting the ranch together. Tina dating Mark had surprised both men, although in the beginning, Aaron had kept his distance.

When Tina had left Mark for Aaron, there had been a part of Mark that hadn't been surprised. Why would she choose him over a guy like Aaron, who had everything Mark didn't?

Mark scowled at the pair as they acted like he was some

charging bull. As if he'd been the one to do something wrong in the first place.

"How are you?" Tina asked. She looked up at Aaron for a brief moment. "It's been a long time," she added softly.

"Mark," Aaron said. He nodded tightly, wary of this little meeting.

Mark was fine with that. He had no interest in being friends again with these two. He also refused to act like he still cared about what had happened. It had been five years, hadn't it? What kind of a man locked himself away for that long because of a past hurt?

"I'm fine. Just getting some feed for my horses."

"We've heard so much about your ranch. How is that going? Do you like it like you always thought you would?" Tina rubbed her belly, probably not even realizing she was doing it.

Seeing her pregnant and married, and to the man she'd cheated on him with? It hurt. It sucked. Mark wanted to find the nearest bar and drink himself into a stupor.

He'd loved Tina beyond anything—beyond what he'd thought was possible for loving a woman. She'd encouraged him to start his ranch and had helped him out of his shell. She'd been his rock, his soulmate, his everything. He'd dreamt of marrying her and having a family with her. He'd even bought her a ring.

And Aaron had been his friend. He'd trusted Aaron like a brother. He still didn't understand how either of them could've done something like that.

"The ranch is fine, thanks for asking," he replied. "I should get back to it."

Aaron gestured toward Mark's arm. "What happened?"

"Fell off a horse."

When Mark didn't offer any more information, Aaron cleared his throat. Tina seemed at a loss.

Although Tina was still beautiful, Mark knew that he didn't long for her like he used to. She didn't have that power over him anymore. And he knew it was because he was no longer in love with her.

This realization startled him, and at the same time, it freed him. Another face came into his vision—the sweet smile of the woman who'd kissed him so passionately yesterday—and his heart clenched for a different reason.

"Since Aaron and I are in town for a bit, would you like to get together?" Tina asked, her tone tentative. "Maybe have a cup of coffee?"

Mark barely restrained a snort. *What the hell would we talk about?* he wondered. He shook his head. "I can't. I have too much going on."

Tina's face fell, and Mark felt guilty, which annoyed him further.

"Have a good afternoon," Mark said.

The pair murmured the same before they walked away, Aaron's arm still around Tina's waist.

"Hey Mark," Caleb called out. He wore his police uniform, a cup of coffee in his hand as he approached. "Was that..?" he asked as he peered into the distance.

Mark's mouth twisted. "Yeah."

Caleb whistled. "Sorry, man. You want to talk about it?"

"When do I ever want to talk about it?"

That made Caleb grin. "Good point. And if I'm being honest, I don't want to talk about it either. Megan makes me talk about my feelings way too much already."

Looking at Caleb, Mark saw that his brother looked more at peace with himself than he had in a long time. Caleb had lived with the guilt of accidentally killing his best friend in a car accident years ago. Although Mark had known part of the story, Caleb had started talking about it only recently. Mark knew this had been due to Megan's influence.

Envy nipped at him. What would it be like to have a woman love you—flaws and all—like that? He thought of Abby, and he had to close his eyes for a second to find his bearings.

"So," Caleb drawled as he leaned against the door of Mark's truck, "I heard that you're dating Abby Davison. The nurse, right?" Caleb cocked an eyebrow. "Considering how you insulted her, I'm dying to hear how you managed that."

Mark suddenly felt very tired. The last thing he wanted to do was explain this bizarre situation of his to his older brother.

"It's complicated. I have to get going."

"Fine, leave. I'll get the details from Megan anyway. You'll be home for Thanksgiving, right? Because if you aren't, Mom will never ever forgive you." His face lit up right then. "Oh, and Lizzie will be in town."

"For real this time?"

Lizzie was a musician who traveled the country with her band. She hadn't been home for at least three years, her excuses ranging from not having time between gigs or not wanting to spend the money. But everybody had a feeling it was a *someone* who kept her away.

"For real this time. She sent Mom her plane ticket info and everything, and you know you can't get those things refunded." Caleb's walkie-talkie sounded; he slapped Mark on the shoulder. "See you later. Don't do anything I wouldn't."

"I'm not that stupid."

Caleb laughed and gave him the bird, making Mark smile for the first time that day.

CHAPTER TEN

Spending a week in Mark's company, Abby somewhat understood his moods and personality. He had never been chatty, but tonight, he was downright surly. He barely spoke more than five words to her all evening, although he did thank her for dinner.

"I just ordered pizza," she said, trying to lighten the mood.

He shrugged.

She sighed. She wanted to shake him until his teeth rattled. At least it would make her feel better, if it didn't get him to talk. They'd gotten so close yesterday afternoon, and now he was acting like she was some kind of stranger.

After they finished eating, Mark said something about finishing up some work outside. Abby squinted, looking at the growing dusk outside.

"What do you have to do right now?" she asked.

She had a feeling he wanted to avoid her. *Can this guy make up his mind already?*

Then again, they weren't in a real relationship. They were...well, Abby didn't know. They were attracted to each other; that wasn't in doubt. This "relationship" was a tangled mess that only got more complicated with each passing day.

"Need to see to the horses," was his curt answer.

She watched him leave without protest. Darcy and Wentworth began to twine around her ankles, purring when she reached down to pet them.

She decided to take a bath and read a book, ignoring Mark for the time being. Around ten, he finally returned inside. She listened as he went to his bedroom and then turned on the water in the master bathroom.

Abby considered. She was, generally speaking, a logical person. She'd enjoyed her encounter with Mark yesterday; she would also like to continue where they'd left off.

Abby had always liked sex, but she'd never felt as blown away by it as she had when Mark had touched her. It had been on a new level. Shivering, she felt her body heat from the memory of his kisses.

So, yes, she wanted him. He wanted her, or he wouldn't have kissed her. They were adults, so if they wanted to have an affair, they should do so without feeling guilty.

But her heart sank into her toes at the thought of something so...arranged. Why could love never enter the bargain? Derek had discarded her without a second thought, especially after he'd found out she couldn't have children.

Her heart twisted when she thought of how she'd never feel a child grow inside her. She'd never call her husband to tell him it was time to go to the hospital. She knew she could adopt, but seeing other women get pregnant and give birth only reminded her that she couldn't.

"I'm not going to sit around and mope," she muttered to

Darcy and Wentworth. Neither cat seemed inclined to offer any support for her predicament—typical.

She wanted to find out what was bothering Mark, even if she had to force it out of him. Knocking on his bedroom door, she waited. When he opened the door, wearing nothing but boxers and no shirt, her mouth watered.

Lord, he was sexy. That was the only word for it. Sexy, handsome, attractive, delicious...all of those things wrapped up in one hot package.

"Abby?" He looked surprised to see her, as if he'd forgotten she was down the hall.

She put her hands on her hips. "What's up with you?" she asked point-blank. She'd discovered the only way to get a real answer from Mark was to be blunt. "You've been acting even weirder than usual tonight."

Mark opened his mouth, closed it. Then he let out a deep breath. "How could you tell?" He opened the door wider.

She hadn't expected him to let her into his room. And now she was here in his bedroom, wearing pajamas while Mark only wore boxers. She flushed at how intimate it felt.

And when he looked at her like he had yesterday afternoon, full of heat and desire? Her heart stuttered.

She didn't know where to sit. Or did she stand? Sitting meant she'd be staying, but standing seemed awkward. She decided to perch on one of the chairs next to the unused fireplace, pulling her robe closed.

So much for having an affair, she thought wryly.

She watched as he slipped on a shirt; he swore a little when he couldn't get his sling through it. She hated that he kept covering that magnificent body in front of her. Then again, she knew she wouldn't be able to concentrate on what he was saying if he were shirtless.

"What happened?" she asked when he sat down.

He looked uncomfortable, which only made her sympathize with him more. "Nothing important," he hedged.

"Uh huh." When he remained silent, she forced the exasperation away.

"When Derek and I were dating," she said into the silence, "he would get upset about something and then refuse to talk about it. I didn't force him to explain, although I wish that I had at least tried. He kept things so bottled up that eventually, he'd explode."

That made Mark look at her. His expression darkened. "Did he—?"

"What? Oh no, nothing like that. He never hurt me. No." *Not physically, anyway.*

She shook off the memory of Derek's painful words. "Point is, talking things through can help. Believe me."

She was a hypocrite, though. Would she tell Mark about how she couldn't have children? How she was afraid that she wasn't worthy of being loved? She didn't know if she'd ever have the courage to tell this secret a second time—even to Mark.

"Why did you guys break up?" Mark asked.

Oh God, she didn't want to talk about this, but what had she just said?

She shrugged. "We dated for four years, and then we grew apart. I decided to end things because he wasn't the right guy for me."

Mark's eyes narrowed. "Sounds like bull."

That startled a laugh out of her. "Does it? If I told you

that he said I wasn't woman enough for him, would you believe that?"

"What the fuck?" he growled, his body tensing. "Why the hell would he say something like that?"

"Because he's an ass." She shrugged, although the old hurt pulsed in her chest. "That's why I broke up with him. Although he wants to get back together now. Weird, right? It's been over a year and suddenly he's realized this?"

She hadn't meant to tell Mark this, but seeing Mark bristle gave her a thrill. Was he actually *jealous?*

Mark scowled. "That guy has more nerve than a fox in a henhouse, and he's a million times more annoying. He must've come to his senses and realized he'll never get a woman better than you. That's why he wants you back."

Her heart lifted at his words. When he seemed to realize what he'd said, Mark rubbed the back of his neck.

Abby hummed. "So, I've talked. Your turn."

He scowled again.

"Don't give me that look. Otherwise I'll never leave this room."

At that declaration, his eyes gleamed. "I wouldn't say no to that," he said in a low voice.

If she was flushed before, now she was an inferno. "Don't change the subject," she replied, ignoring how breathy she sounded. "Tell me what happened."

"Spoilsport." He inhaled deeply; he grimaced. Then: "I saw my ex today."

Abby's eyebrows rose. "Seems to be a running theme with us."

He laughed a little. "I guess. She was with her husband, and she was pregnant."

Now Abby was in delicate territory. "Is she the woman in the photo?" she asked quietly.

"Yeah, but..." Rising, he went to his dresser and pulled out the photo in question. Before Abby could react, he ripped the photo in two. Then fours, and then it was mere confetti that he tossed into the nearby trash can.

He turned back to Abby. "I should've done that years ago. I don't know why I kept that photo of Tina, because seeing her today reminded me that I'd fallen out of love with her a long time ago."

Abby's heart pounded so hard she felt dizzy. He didn't love Tina anymore. He'd torn up that photo without a second thought.

Desire pulsed inside her, throbbing in her veins. She wanted Mark with an intensity that she'd never felt before for any man.

She rose as he approached her. She only came up to his shoulder. He made her feel impossibly small, yet protected.

And the look in his eyes? It was filled with so much heat that Abby felt scorched.

"I don't want to talk about our exes anymore," he rumbled. He touched her hair with gentle fingers.

She swallowed. "What do you want to talk about?"

"Nothing." He brushed her bottom lip with his thumb. "I only want to make you mine."

Abby struggled for breath. He traced her lip with his thumb, and that light touch sent her pulse into overdrive.

"Tell me you want to stay, Abby." Mark cupped her cheek. "Or I'll let you go and never ask you again."

She trembled. "Yes, I want to stay," she said without hesitation.

His eyes flared before he kissed her. They both moaned long and low at the contact. He was all heat and strength, even with his broken arm pressing against her side. When he slicked his tongue inside her mouth, she felt light-headed.

The man could kiss, she'd give him that. He kissed to seduce, to captivate. Abby couldn't get enough, and when she felt him squeeze her ass, she dug her fingers harder into his shoulder.

"Take this off," he said, tugging on her robe. "I want to see you."

"Only if you do the same."

They both undressed at the same time, although Mark took longer with his broken arm. Abby almost offered to help, but the look in his eyes told her that he wouldn't appreciate the blow to his manhood.

Mark may have seen her topless yesterday, but getting completely naked in front of him? It was a huge step for her, as she usually requested that the lights were off during sex.

Anxiety and excitement filled her in equal measures. Her hands shook as she pushed her pajamas shorts and panties down before slipping off her tank.

Mark stripped out of his boxers, his cock half-hard already. Her breath quickened. Dark hair covered his chest, arrowing down his torso to his groin. Those muscles rippled as he moved, like a wild cat.

Abby could see how tight his expression was and how his nostrils flared as he stared at her. She felt powerful, like some kind of goddess. Her anxiety melted away.

No woman could remain self-conscious with a man like Mark looking at her like she was the only thing he'd ever wanted.

Trailing her fingers down his torso, feeling the springy hair, she smiled. She'd missed this: this closeness with a man. Touching a man, tasting him.

Standing on her tiptoes, she kissed him, sweeping her tongue along the seam of his lips. He tangled his fingers in her hair with a groan, tipping her head back to give him better access.

As they kissed, she wrapped her hand around his cock, now fully erect. He let out another groan as she gripped him. She learned this part of him, the sight of which set her body aflame. At first she stroked him with a light touch, but before long he covered her hand with his own.

"Harder," he breathed against her mouth. "Like this."

They gripped him together for a few more moments, and she felt him grow larger against her palm. Her body pulsed. The smell of sex and salt filled the room, and Abby wanted to lick the scent from his skin.

But Mark broke the embrace with a muttered oath. "Get on the bed."

He headed to the bathroom, leaving Abby standing in the middle of his room.

Climbing onto the bed, she wondered if she should get under the covers or not. She was already warm, but the thought of lying naked on top of Mark's sheets seemed almost too brazen for her. She decided to compromise by pushing the comforter to the foot of the bed and getting under the sheets, which cooled her overheated body.

When Mark returned, all thoughts of sheets and comforters fled her mind. She saw the gleam of foil packets in his hand, and he tossed the condoms onto the nightstand before climbing into bed with her. When he saw the sheet covering her, he grinned.

"Shy?" he murmured. He kissed her shoulder, moving her hair aside.

She inhaled as he licked her. "No," she breathed, because it was true. She didn't feel shy around him because he'd never given her a reason to feel shy in the first place.

He pushed the sheet down until her breasts were bared, and she wiggled out from under the covers with a laugh. Like they'd done yesterday afternoon, Abby straddled Mark while sitting on his lap. He was strong, but even he couldn't keep his weight only on his good arm if he were on top.

This also gave her a chance to keep kissing him and exploring him. His cock pressed against her belly, hot and hard. His own hands were busy, stroking down her spine, feeling each vertebrae in her back. When he found her sex, already wet for him, he groaned.

"Goddamn, Abby. I never thought—" He shook his head as he dipped a finger inside her sheath.

Abby gasped as he played with her, spreading her moisture over her folds, pressing and petting and driving her wild. She bucked against his hand, begging for more pressure, saying his name like a litany.

Her climax built with stunning speed, but then he moved his fingers away. She whimpered in protest.

"I can't wait any longer." He reached for a condom, only to make an annoyed noise when he realized he couldn't get a packet with his good arm. "Goddammit."

She leaned over and plucked one off the nightstand, smiling as she ripped it open. "I think I can manage to do this. Unless you think I need instructions?"

He laughed, but then he groaned when she began to roll the condom down his length. She couldn't stop herself from giving him one last squeeze, which made him tug at her hair.

Her heart started pounding hard when she rose onto her knees, taking his cock in her hand. They both moaned when the tip began to breach her.

Slowly—savoring every inch—Abby sank down on him, her eyes widening at how he filled her. Her nails dug into his shoulders, which made him groan.

She watched his face the entire time. Seeing the flush on his cheeks, the way his eyes had darkened? How his hand shook on her lower back? It was overwhelming.

Closing her eyes for a moment, she had to gain control of herself as she took him inside of her. He was so big, so much bigger than she'd had before that it was almost too much.

Mark waited, but she knew his control was about to splinter. Opening her eyes, she started to move, his cock filling her until she started to gasp, pleasure tightening in her belly.

Mark's hand tightened on her waist a moment before he lay on his back on the bed, his knees against Abby's back. This gave him the leverage he needed, and he began to piston inside her. Abby bit back a scream.

Sweat beaded on her forehead and between her breasts. She held on as he used her for his own pleasure, lost in his frenzy. And she *loved* it. Her release trembled at the edges of her consciousness, and when she reached down to rub her clit, she bit her lip so hard she tasted blood.

When he saw that she was touching herself, he swore. He thrust even harder, and the combined sensation of his cock pounding inside her and her finger rubbing her clit was too much. She shattered with a keening cry, her body shaking.

Mark wrapped his arm around her as he thrust once, twice, three more times, and then he yelled with his own release. Abby felt his cock twitch inside her. Euphoria flooded her in waves.

They both collapsed onto his bed, sweaty and sated.

"Are you okay?" Mark asked, his gaze concerned. He pushed her hair from her forehead.

How could she answer that question? Her body was boneless, but her heart felt like it had splintered. She murmured something noncommittal before she snuggled against his side.

Mark fell asleep within moments, but Abby remained awake for some time. She wished she could ignore this pain in her chest.

Was she okay? She was no longer sure of the answer.

CHAPTER ELEVEN

Mark awoke right as dawn stretched its fingers through the curtains, coating his room in golden light. It took him a moment to orient himself: he was in his room, yes, but there was a warm weight snuggled next to him.

He looked down to see Abby fast asleep with her head on his shoulder. She made a noise and turned over, giving him a magnificent view of her backside.

Biting back a groan, he moved her fully off of his shoulder as gently as he could and rose from the bed. He knew she needed to get up for work soon. He got her phone from her room, knowing it had her alarm programed; he set it on the nightstand, watching her sleep for a moment.

They'd had sex last night. He almost wondered if it had been a dream, but no, his body was too satisfied for it to have been a dream. Closing his eyes, he remembered Abby's face as she came, how she felt when she rode him. It had been a while since he'd slept with a woman, but this?

This couldn't compare. And now all he wanted was to have her—again and again and again.

As he went into the kitchen, he felt something soft brushing against his legs. Abby's two cats twined around his ankles, mewing softly. The one with the white patch stood on its hind legs and was about to dig its claws into Mark's knee.

He bent down to pet them. "You guys hungry? Come on."

The cats meowed and followed him, and then they meowed even louder as he wondered how much food to give them. He'd never owned a cat before. If he gave them too much, would they get sick like a dog would?

The cats almost tripped him as he dumped a cup of cat food in each of their bowls. He watched them eat, surprised to see that they both ate only half of what was in their bowls. *So much for being worried.*

When he began to make something for breakfast, Abby came into the kitchen. She smiled at him, which was a good sign. If she acted like she'd regretted what had happened last night, he didn't know how he'd react.

They got their own breakfasts in silence, but when they brushed against each other, the electricity sizzled between them. When Abby bent over to get something out of a cabinet, Mark had to look away from her round backside in the air.

"I fed your cats," he said.

She looked at the bowls still filled with food; she seemed to bite back a smile. "How much did you give them?"

"Enough."

"Thank you, then. They can be annoying when they're hungry."

They sat down at the table and began to eat, Abby with a bowl of cereal while Mark ate toast with some bacon. He wracked his brain to think of something to say.

Last night was great?

Do you want to do it again?

I can't stop thinking about how you look naked?

None of those seemed like appropriate breakfast conversations.

Abby was the one to break the silence. After taking a drink of her coffee, she said, "I was thinking. About last night."

He watched in amusement as pink tinged her cheeks, and he barely restrained himself from teasing her. *Since when do I tease people?* He wasn't exactly Mr. Funny Man like his brother Caleb.

"I had a good time last night, but I think we should talk about what happened, you know?"

Hell no, he thought, but he bit into his toast instead. Why did women always want to talk about things? Couldn't they have sex, enjoy it, and go on with their days without analyzing every second of it?

"I had a good time, too," he replied, feeling out of his depth for the millionth time around this woman.

"I'd like to continue with our—relationship." Abby cleared her throat. "But I think we should be clear that it's just sex. Nothing else."

Mark hadn't expected the disappointment. Had he thought she'd want anything else besides sex? *And why is that a bad thing anyway?*

"So this is an affair. No feelings." He leaned back in his chair. "That's what I'd always assumed it was," he lied.

If he saw a tiny crease of hurt in her features, well, he'd probably imagined it.

She nodded. "Good, then it's settled. We enjoy this while it lasts, but with no other expectations."

"I won't keep paying you, though. And you don't need to help me around the house." At her surprised look, he flushed. "I mean, I can pay you if you want, it just seems..."

Her lips quirked. "You don't need to explain. I agree. Although I wouldn't say no to you paying for my gas still."

That made him laugh. "I can do that. It's a deal then."

They shook on it, but Mark couldn't stop himself from kissing her. She giggled and pushed him away after a few deep kisses, breathlessly saying she needed to get ready for work.

As Mark worked on the ranch, Charlie seemed to notice that he was surlier than usual, but he was wise enough not to say anything.

Women never failed to tie a man up in knots. He muttered to himself as he brushed down the horses, Delilah nudging him on the shoulder when he stopped brushing her.

Well, if sex was all Abby wanted? He'd give it to her. He vowed that they'd have the best damn sex on the planet.

Days passed, and as autumn faded and winter closed in, Abby and Mark's arrangement continued as planned. She lived with him, they had mind-blowing sex, and there were no feelings involved whatsoever.

By mid-November, the leaves had fallen from the trees, the landscape bare and the weather chilly. Rain fell most days, and sometimes it rained so hard that Abby wondered how Mark got anything done on the ranch with all of the mud.

Delilah's due date also approached, and the veterinarian had visited and pronounced both her and her foal healthy.

"She's young and strong," Mark had explained to Abby after the vet had left. "But I can't help but worry."

Abby knew he loved that horse more than anyone else on this earth, which might be insulting if she had feelings for him. Which she did not.

Just because she missed him while she was at work, or longed for him the nights he had to stay overnight on some work-related trip? That didn't mean she had feelings for him. It was because she missed the sex.

A week before Thanksgiving, Mark came home from a doctor's appointment and said, "I get my cast off on Monday. Thank God."

Abby stirred the chili, not sure how to respond. Their original arrangement had been that she stayed here until his arm healed. But their arrangement had changed already, hadn't it? She was no longer getting paid to help him, although she still cooked most days because she enjoyed cooking. Otherwise, she'd remained because she didn't want their affair to end.

How did my life get so complicated? she thought morosely.

"That's good. I'm glad it's healing so well," she replied, trying to sound chipper. "Are you going home for Thanksgiving?"

Mark grunted, which she'd learned meant "yes, but I'm not happy about it" in Mark Language.

"Actually, I wanted to talk to you about that. Do you want to come with me?" he asked.

"What? You mean go to your parents' house?"

"Yeah. They want to meet you, since we're supposed to be dating. Or whatever it is we're doing."

Her shoulders slumped. This was about keeping up

appearances, wasn't it? Everyone thought they were still dating, and if she intended to stay here, it would make sense to continue the charade. Her head started to hurt from thinking about it all.

"Well, if you think it's a good idea," she hedged as she moved past him to get some spices, "I'll go. Your family is famous enough that seeing them at Thanksgiving will at least be interesting."

"That's one way to put it. I promise my mom will be on her best behavior. She's been on probation ever since she messed around with Harrison and Sara."

Abby knew all about that story from Megan. When Harrison and Sara had started dating, Lisa Thornton had tried to interfere, refusing to believe a trashy Flannigan girl was good enough for her oldest son. To say that Harrison had been angry would be an understatement.

"That doesn't sound at all intimidating," Abby joked.

Mark smiled. "My mom will be too interested in talking about Harrison's wedding. Or when Caleb's getting engaged. Or about my sister Lizzie—she'll be home for the first time in a while."

Now Abby was doubly intrigued. "Lizzie? Isn't she a musician?"

"Yeah. If our mother hates that I own a ranch, she probably hates that Lizzie is a musician even more."

Abby tasted the chili and after adding a little more salt, she turned the burner down to low. "Your mom is certainly...memorable."

"That's one way to put it." His face creased a little as he asked, "So you really will come?"

She should say no. Wasn't this only entangling herself

further? To meet his family like this? But the other choice was to go to her aunt's place with her mom, where her relatives would grill her about her new relationship. At least at the Thorntons', she'd have a chance of hanging in the background.

"Sure, I'll come."

Mark smiled, his eyes creasing at the corners, and the sight of it hit Abby right in the chest.

Had she really told him that there wouldn't be any feelings involved?

She was such a liar.

When Mark wrapped his arms around her as she washed dishes, she closed her eyes. His touch caused both pleasure and pain now, her emotions in knots.

He trailed kisses down her neck, and she pressed against him, feeling his arousal.

"Do the dishes later," he growled. He nipped at her earlobe.

"Only if you're doing them."

He laughed, husky and low. "Deal." He turned her around and kissed her. She wrapped her arms around his neck, needing to get closer.

When had Mark Thornton become so necessary to me?

They stumbled to his bedroom, laughing when Abby almost tripped over a cat. Collapsing onto the bed together, they kissed desperately, the mood heating until it was almost explosive.

She scratched her nails down his back, feeling him shudder. He rolled over, taking her with him so she was on top. His broken arm had prevented him from being on top. She hadn't complained, but she did wonder what it would be like to have Mark above her, dominating her as he moved inside her.

They stripped out of their clothes. Abby gripped his cock, rubbing him with sure strokes, but he pushed her hands away within moments. He tugged on one of her legs, motioning for her to move to the edge of the bed. He kneeled on the floor and placed her feet on his shoulders, opening her up to him.

She tangled her fingers in his hair as he kissed down her torso. She bit back a cry as he swirled his tongue in her belly button.

He slid his fingers through her soaked folds, and he said her name in a low rumble. As they kept eye contact, he pushed a finger inside her and then another, stretching her. A rush of wetness flooded from her body.

"Yes, Mark, yes," she murmured. She arched and bucked, all sense of modesty long since discarded. When he licked her, she gasped. He played with her like this until she was a quivering mess. Her orgasm came closer and closer.

When he hooked his fingers upward, moving them faster and faster inside her tightening sheath, that pressure combined with his tongue circling her clit drove her insane. Panting for breath, her release burst upon her.

Screaming, she clutched at his head, her heels digging into his back. Her vision went black. Collapsing onto the bed, still quivering, she watched as Mark went to the nightstand to get a condom. He tore it open with his teeth, his gaze hot as he looked at her.

Abby sat up as he climbed onto the bed. He stroked down her torso, turning her over so she faced away from him. She let out a breathless laugh when he smacked her ass.

He lay down behind her, resting on his good arm. He kissed the back of her neck, licking her and biting.

Abby couldn't wait any longer. Lifting her leg so it rested on his hip, she reached for his engorged length with eager fingers. She gripped him and stroked him a few times; he bit her nape harder when she squeezed him at the base.

"Put me inside you," he growled.

But she played with him a little longer, cupping his balls, her hands wandering. He swore and bucked. There wasn't anything quite so heady as having this strong man in her power.

When his cock pressed against her entrance, she moaned, long and low. As she sank onto him, they both gasped. Abby's vision blurred, and her entire body twitched as Mark began to thrust.

At this angle, his thrusts were shallow, but they hit a spot inside her that drove her wild. She pressed against his chest, trying to get even closer; she turned her head so they could kiss. It was awkward and messy, but it was also the most erotic thing Abby had ever experienced. His tongue thrust in her mouth as his cock filled her.

Tendrils of ecstasy began to coil around her. It was unbearable, almost painful. Her fingers twitched on the covers.

Mark went faster, and she could feel his sweat on her back. Closing her eyes, she felt her second release rushing toward her until finally she burst.

She shook and screamed, and then she heard him say her name as he reached his peak a few thrusts later. He swore, groaning, and she wished she could see his expression as he came.

Abby couldn't move after that. She was pretty sure her bones had melted. Mark took care of the condom before climbing back into bed beside Abby.

When he curled his good arm around her, she felt close to tears.

She'd said there wouldn't be any feelings? What a lie. A big, fat, hilarious lie.

CHAPTER TWELVE

Abby's mouth fell open as she took in the Thornton mansion. And it was definitely a mansion, with its endless driveway leading up to a house that could be photographed for some magazine. How many rooms did this place have? She almost didn't want to know.

When Abby had mentioned going to the Thornton Thanksgiving, Fiona had been adamant that her daughter not get cold feet.

"I'm going to my sister's, anyway," she'd said, "so you have no excuse. But you have to tell me all about those Thorntons afterward!"

So this is how rich people live. She couldn't help but compare this palace with her own small apartment.

Mark escorted her inside, and Abby clutched her purse. Butterflies fluttered in her stomach, although whether they were from Mark's touch or from the wealth surrounding her, she wasn't sure.

"Oh good, you're here!" Megan rushed toward Abby and enveloped her in a fierce hug. "Sara and Harrison aren't here yet, and I was going to have to talk to Lisa alone because Caleb is the *worst.*" Seeing Mark standing there, Megan grinned. "Hey, Mark. How's it going? How are your pigs?"

Seeing Abby's confused look, Mark explained in a dry voice, "Some people like to joke that I raise pigs. They think it's funny."

"It *is* funny," Megan said. She then narrowed her eyes at Mark.

Although Abby had told Megan about the "arrangement," Abby hadn't told Mark that she'd told Megan.

Abby gave Megan a warning look.

"Let's go to the living—no, wait, *sitting* room," Megan said. She took Abby's arm, her eyes gleaming. "I want to hear about everything since we last talked."

To Abby's surprise, no one was in the sitting room. The trio chatted, Abby updating her friend without disclosing too much, while Megan tried to get Mark to talk, albeit in vain.

"Hey everybody!" Caleb exclaimed. He slapped Mark on the back, which Mark returned.

A woman Abby had never seen before followed behind Caleb. Her dark hair and green eyes marked her immediately as a Thornton, though.

"Abby, this is our prodigal sister Lizzie," Caleb said. "This is Abby Davison, Mark's girlfriend. She's a nurse at Fair Haven Memorial."

Abby shook Lizzie's hand, and the woman smiled at her warmly. She was beautiful, with her golden skin and dark hair that rippled down her back in waves. She was tall and stylish, wearing jeans that hugged every curve.

Mark rose, and Lizzie hugged him hard. "How are you, you big lug?" she said. "How's the ranch? And your horses?"

He smiled. "Good. You could come see them all, you know."

"True. Maybe I will." Turning to Abby, she said, "How has he been behaving? He hasn't growled at you too many times, has he?"

"Lizzie," Mark warned.

Everyone laughed. Lizzie bantered with Caleb and Megan, and before long, more guests arrived. Harrison and Sara came with Sara's son James, along with Jubilee. Heath DiMarco, Harrison and Caleb's best friend, arrived after that. Ruth Flannigan, Sara and Megan's mother, had gone to visit her brother in eastern Washington.

As the conversation flowed around them, Abby leaned over to whisper in Mark's ear, "Where are your parents?"

"Mom's probably having a stroke over the turkey while my dad is hiding," he whispered back.

When Lisa Thornton came into the sitting room, she didn't look like she'd had a stroke. In fact, she looked as calm and collected as a woman with a house full of guests could be. In her late fifties, Lisa remained an attractive woman, although she had an iciness to her that made her seem deliberately standoffish.

Dave Thornton was the spitting image of his sons, only with gray hair and a lined face.

"Mark, introduce me to your girlfriend," Lisa said.

Abby stood up, not wanting this woman to loom over her. It helped her confidence somewhat that Lisa was only an inch taller than her.

"Mom, Dad, this is Abby Davison. Abby, meet my parents, Lisa and Dave."

Abby shook Lisa's hand and then Dave's. Lisa inspected

her with a critical eye, while Dave seemed disinterested at best. They both said the usual greetings and then turned to the rest of their children.

Abby sat back down and let out the breath she hadn't realized she'd been holding.

"That wasn't so bad," she said.

Mark's lips twisted. "My mom's trying."

Right then, Sara's son James plopped down between Abby and Mark.

"You're the nurse who helped Caleb, right?" James asked. "I've seen you before."

"That's right. And you're James?"

"Yeah." He turned his gaze toward Mark. "You look like Harrison."

"I'm his brother," Mark said, his tone serious. "His younger brother."

"His name is Mark." Abby smiled at Mark over James's head.

"I knew that," James replied, sounding exasperated. "I've been to dinner and Mark was there. He has horses but my mom says I'm too young to ride a horse."

He returned to grilling Mark. "What's it like to have brothers? I told my mom she should give me a younger brother but she always tells me to go outside."

Abby had to bite the inside of her cheek to keep from laughing, while Mark looked like he'd rather be anywhere else.

"Brothers are a total pain. I have two older brothers and one younger brother." Mark shrugged, smiling a little. "But I'd miss them if they weren't around."

After James peppered them both with more questions, Sara came to get her son.

"Sorry, I hope he wasn't bothering you." Sara gave James a stern look. "You know what I said about bothering people, right?"

James sighed. "I know, but they didn't say I was bothering them."

"It's fine. James asks good questions," Abby said.

Abby's heart twisted a little as James went to go sit with Sara. Would she ever have a child of her own?

Most days, she didn't mind being around kids—it wasn't like she could avoid children as a nurse—but sometimes the pang of longing hit her at the oddest times. Living with Mark had brought a lot of those longings to the surface.

Dinner was served shortly thereafter. The dining room table was set with every Thanksgiving delicacy imaginable: mashed potatoes, gravy, rolls of bread, green beans, candied yams. The turkey sat at the end of the table, fried to golden perfection.

Abby inhaled the scents of butter and turkey, her stomach rumbling. If all else failed, at least the food would be delicious.

Abby found her seat with her place card, her name written in calligraphy. She realized she'd sit with Mark on her right and Lizzie on her left. Lizzie gave her a kind smile as she sat down next to her.

Dave carved the turkey before everyone began to fill their plates with food. As Abby took a platter of candied yams from Lizzie, she couldn't help but ask, "I heard you're a musician?"

"That's right. I tour with my band, so that's why I haven't been home in a while."

"That sounds exciting, though. What kind of music is it?"

"I like to call us an indie band," Lizzie explained as she placed some mashed potatoes onto her plate. "I'm the lead singer. We do a lot of atmospheric kind of songs, I guess. I'm terrible at describing it. You just have to listen to it, is what I always say."

"She's trying to get you to buy her album," Mark interjected in a wry voice. "Don't fall for it, Abby."

Lizzie laughed. "He's right, kind of, although I am terrible at describing what kind of music we perform."

"Have you always been a musician?" Abby asked.

"For the most part. I think I wanted to be a vet for a few years as a kid, but music is my first love." Lizzie took a sip of her wine, her expression faraway for a moment. "Music has always been a part of me."

"I'd love to hear you sing one day."

"I'm actually doing a show here in town in a few weeks. You should come."

"I'd love to, thank you."

She turned to see Mark watching her. Suddenly embarrassed that she'd ignored him, she said, "The food's great."

"It is."

She struggled with what she should say. Since when did she get tongue-tied around Mark? She told herself it was because she was around his entire family; they made her self-conscious.

Or it's because his family thinks that you're in a relationship with Mark when you're just having sex with a man you might be falling for.

Abby's thoughts scattered when Lisa began to grill her children. "Sara told me that you picked out a date for the wedding," she said to Harrison, "but are you sure about getting married outside then? June can still be so wet. I'm worried you'll get rained out."

Harrison looked like the last thing he wanted to do was

talk about his and Sara's wedding, but then James piped in. "They can use umbrellas if it rains. That's what I do."

Everyone laughed, which helped break the tension.

Sara said, "We thought about that, but we don't want to wait any longer, so June it is."

"I went to a wedding years ago—Dave, remember the Patterson wedding?—and they had it outside in *April*. April! Everyone was soaked to the skin, and I swear I almost got pneumonia."

"We promise no one will contract pneumonia at our wedding," Harrison said, deadpan.

Caleb snorted, which made Megan elbow him.

Lisa glared at Caleb before saying, "And what about you, Caleb? When will you finally ask Megan to marry you?"

That made Caleb choke on his water. "Jesus, Mom, give a guy some warning!"

"Language." Lisa dabbed at her lips with her napkin. "Answer the question."

Caleb looked rather like a deer in the headlights, and he looked at Megan, and then his siblings, for help. Megan patted his shoulder.

"We just haven't gotten that far yet," Megan explained. "We just moved in together."

That caused exclamations around the table, although Abby noted that Lisa didn't take the news quite as well. She seemed miffed, like they were moving in together only to annoy her.

"I amend my previous statement. Your mother is terrifying," Abby whispered to Mark.

The conversation shifted from weddings and engagements to Jubilee's job working at Megan's bakery. Lisa asked Jubilee what her future plans were, Jubilee taking the question with aplomb. Abby could imagine that she was used to her mother's constant grilling.

Abby soon noticed that Heath was gazing at Jubilee. Abby didn't know Heath well. He worked at the elementary school and had been friends with Harrison and Caleb for a while.

Tonight, he'd worn dress pants and a button-up shirt, his auburn hair slicked back. He wore glasses, but it only gave him an air of sophistication. He was handsome, albeit unassuming, especially compared to the overt handsomeness of the Thornton men.

But apparently, Heath only had eyes for Jubilee. *Interesting.*

When Heath caught Abby looking at him, he didn't react. His gaze drifted away and back to his plate.

"I can't believe anyone but family would come to these dinners," Lizzie said as she leaned over toward Abby. "How did Mark convince you to come? Did he blackmail you?"

Abby almost choked on her wine. *You have no idea,* she thought.

"Can I admit that I was curious?" she whispered back.

Lizzie grinned. "You sound like my kind of girl. Megan wants us all to go out one night, mostly to commiserate about how obnoxious the Thornton men are. You should come."

Abby nodded, a tightness filling her chest. She hated that she was lying to these people, who'd welcomed her into their home and treated her like a real family member. She even felt guilty about lying to Lisa, of all people.

After dinner, the family returned to the sitting room, where drinks flowed in abundance. James was all energy, going from adult to adult, until Harrison took him outside to play catch, Heath and Jubilee joining the pair.

"I need to work off those mashed potatoes," Jubilee said cheerfully. "Come on, James, teach me how to throw a ball because I'm terrible at it."

James proceeded to tell Jubilee that that was because she was a *girl*, with Jubilee disclaiming this assertion heatedly.

Abby got up to get another glass of wine, Mark joining her. He poured her glass before pouring a snifter of whiskey for himself.

"Thanks for coming tonight," he said quietly.

She looked up in surprise. "Of course."

"Really. I know my family isn't—easy."

Her lips twitched. "You said it, not me."

He laughed as they returned to the couch.

MARK WATCHED his family in silence. Abby was like an anchor for his sanity. Having her near had made being around his family easier than usual.

"Hey everybody, I have a surprise," Lizzie announced. She motioned to Caleb, who turned on the flat-screen TV.

"Are we watching football for once?" Dave asked. Since having a few glasses of wine, he'd become almost jovial.

Lisa sniffed. "You know how I feel about football. What is this all about, Elizabeth?"

"One sec..." She and Caleb plugged in a laptop and then a microphone. "Hey, can someone go get everybody from outside? They'll want to be here, too."

"I'll do it," Mark said.

Mark watched Harrison and Heath toss a football to James, who then tried to run off with it. Jubilee caught him, and he squealed. She then stole the ball and began to run in the opposite direction.

"Get her! Get her!" James cried. Heath ran after her, his long legs catching up to her within moments.

When he snagged an arm around her waist, pulling her into his embrace, Mark waited for them to part. They didn't.

It may have only been a second, but he'd be insane not to see the blush on Jubi's cheeks, or how Heath finally let her go like she'd burnt him.

Mark's eyes narrowed. *Interesting—and definitely a problem.* He'd need to talk to his brothers about this little development. Jubilee was too young for a guy like Heath.

Harrison, though, was distracted with James, and after Mark told them to come inside, he forgot about that little scene for now.

He wasn't going to let any guy take advantage of Jubi. She'd been through enough already.

When they returned to the sitting room, Lizzie glowed with excitement.

"Okay, is everyone ready? Let's get this party started."

A moment later, Lizzie's twin Seth appeared on the screen. He was currently stationed overseas in the Marines.

"Seth!" the family exclaimed in unison. Mark saw his mother's mouth open in surprise, and then she dabbed at her eyes.

Seth smiled and waved at everyone.

"Seth, can you hear us?" Lizzie asked.

"I can hear you."

"Good, we can hear you, too. How are you? When are you coming home?"

Seth looked a lot like his brothers, but with his buzz cut and his deep tan, he looked rougher, even more than Mark.

Mark hadn't seen his little brother since he'd been on leave two years ago, and he couldn't help but notice that Seth looked older, grimmer. It was in his eyes, Mark thought.

Lizzie and Seth, being twins, had been inseparable growing up, and they'd gotten into a whole host of trouble along the way. But right when they were about to graduate high school, something had happened to cause a rift between them.

Although based on Lizzie's happiness right now, Mark had a feeling the rift had finally begun to heal.

Abby had stayed on the couch as the rest of the family crowded around the laptop.

"Let me introduce you," Mark said as he motioned to Abby.

"Hey Seth," he called out, "this is Abby Davison." He swallowed, hoping nobody caught him in his lie. "My girlfriend."

Seth's brows rose a little. "Nice to meet you. Sorry I couldn't come in person."

"When will you be home for good?" Lisa asked. "I hate having my babies scattered all over the world."

"That's why I asked Lizzie to set this up. I'll be on leave again for Christmas and will be home through New Year's."

Everyone shouted in excitement.

"All of the Thornton siblings, back together again," Caleb said with a laugh. "That'll be fun."

Seth gave them an update, although it was vague in the details. Mark couldn't imagine what his little brother had seen out there.

"We miss you," Lizzie said right before they disconnected. "We can't wait to see you."

"Miss you too, Lizard." He smiled. "Don't do anything stupid while I'm gone?"

"Never. Just come home safely, okay?"

By this point, James was yawning and about to fall asleep, and Mark wanted to go home with Abby for some peace and quiet. He could only take so much of his family in one evening.

When Abby didn't return from the bathroom after almost fifteen minutes, Mark went to look for her, concerned that something was wrong. Or that Lisa had cornered her.

He found her outside, gazing at the sunset, her arms wrapped around herself.

"Are you okay?" he asked.

She jumped a little, and when she faced him, he could see her eyes sparkling with tears. He'd wring his mother's neck if she had hurt Abby's feelings.

"What is it? Did my mom—?"

Abby shook her head. "No, no, your mom's done nothing. She was even nice to me earlier." But Abby wiped at her eyes and sighed.

Now Mark was at a loss. He struggled to say what he should, or if he even had a right to pry. *Did you ask about these things with the woman you were having an affair with?*

"Now I'm confused," he muttered.

"I feel so guilty, you know? Lying to your family like this." Abby rubbed her arms. "I kept wanting to tell everyone the truth. And then meeting your brother Seth, who's fighting for our country... I feel like a fraud."

"You aren't a fraud," he said swiftly. "If anything, blame me. I was the one who asked you to come."

Her eyes widened, and then she leaned her forehead against his chest. "Mark..."

He couldn't find the words, so instead, he kissed her, tasting salt on her lips. He was lost in Abby for long moments, not even hearing the screen door opening.

Someone cleared their throat. Mark broke the kiss, but he didn't let Abby go. He looked over his shoulder to see Lizzie.

"Sorry to interrupt, but Sara and Harrison are leaving. I thought you'd want to say goodbye," she said.

"Thanks, Liz," Mark replied.

Lizzie gave them a small smile and left them alone again.

Abby moved away, leaving Mark feeling bereft.

"We should go soon," she said quietly. "It's been a long day."

He wanted to say something, anything, but what could he say? He'd never been good with words. He flailed like a trout upon dry land.

"You aren't a fraud," he repeated. He clenched his jaw, trying to say the right thing. "You might not be my girlfriend, but you aren't just some woman, either."

Her eyes shone. To his surprise, she didn't say anything, but merely kissed him before turning to go inside.

CHAPTER THIRTEEN

The Sunday following Thanksgiving, Mark came inside the house to tell Abby that he thought that Delilah was in labor. Excitement laced his voice, and Abby couldn't help but get excited, too.

"Should we do anything? Call the vet?" she asked.

"No, her pregnancy has been healthy. The best thing we can do is leave her alone. Horses don't like to be disturbed when giving birth."

Abby smiled wryly. "Can't say that I blame her."

Mark stayed outside, working with Charlie as the day passed, trying his best not to hover over Delilah. He'd check on her and then give Abby updates.

After Abby had gotten the last update from Mark, she decided to go to bed, hopeful that in the morning, there'd be an adorable new foal to coo over.

When she heard the knock on her bedroom door, she had to rub the edges of sleep from her eyes. She looked at the clock, which said three-thirty am.

"Abby? I need your help," Mark said from the doorway.

She turned on a lamp, blinking at the sudden wash of light. "What is it?"

"It's Delilah. Something's wrong. I think it's the placenta." His expression was grim, his complexion white. "I've called the vet, but he's an hour away."

She was about to ask what *she* could do, but her nurse's training kicked in automatically. At least she could keep Mark calm while they waited for the vet.

"I'll be right there," she said as she grabbed her jeans.

In the barn, Delilah lay on the stall floor, her breathing labored. Mark beckoned Abby inside the stall.

"I think the placenta detached early," he said. He crouched down, stroking Delilah's head. He gestured at the horse. "Can you look at her?"

Abby put up her hands. "Mark, I'm not a vet."

"I know, but you're the best we've got right now." At her hesitation, he took her hand. "Please," he pleaded.

She nodded, praying she could help somehow. As she began to examine Delilah, she made sure not to move too quickly and startle her. Looking at the horse's vulva, she saw what looked like a red bag, a telltale sign of the placenta detaching too soon.

She'd seen placental abruptions before in humans, and she'd been in the delivery room when a pregnant woman had come into the ER complaining of excessive bleeding before they'd discovered the cause.

"We need surgical scissors—something to cut away the placenta." She knew very well what would happen if they waited too long to deliver the foal: like a human baby experiencing the same issue, the foal would die from a lack of oxygen.

She washed her hands as best as she could and put on gloves while Mark did the same.

Before they returned to the stall, he said, "Thank you, Abby. Whatever happens, thank you."

She wanted to hug him, but they didn't have time. When they returned, Delilah was snorting, clearly in distress as she tried to push the foal from her body. Mark soothed her while Abby began to work.

She prayed again that she could save this foal, or at the very least, save Delilah. Her hands shaking a little, she cut open the red part of the placenta. She saw hooves and what looked like the foal's front feet.

"Is its front feet supposed to come first?" she asked, unsure.

Mark nodded. "One foot, then the other, then its head."

"Can you come help me?" She then cut through the white part of the placenta to allow the foal to pass through. Her heart pounded, but she stayed steady, thankful for her years in the ER.

Working with Mark, they managed to get one foot out. Delilah had another contraction, which pushed out the second foot. A few moments later, the head emerged. Mark and Abby stood back to let Delilah finish birthing the foal.

The foal came out in a gush of fluid, and Abby let out a relieved breath that it was delivered finally. She cut the umbilical cord, checking to make sure the entire placenta had been expelled.

Although she wasn't an expert in horse anatomy, she could make a fairly good estimate that the placenta had emerged completely and that Delilah was out of danger.

"We should watch the foal for hypoxia," Abby explained.

The foal sat on the stall floor, wet and rather pathetic-looking, but it seemed all right. Abby didn't know what to expect, though. She let out a relieved breath when the foal started to stand on its spindly legs.

Mark looked like he was about to collapse. Abby led him out of the stall to sit on a bench so they both could catch their breaths.

She felt tears prick her eyes, and the tears only increased at the look of relief and joy on Mark's face.

"We did it," she said.

Mark smiled. "*You* did it. You saved both of them. You kept your head when I couldn't."

"I am a nurse." But she flushed a little at his praise.

"No, you're—you're amazing." His eyes brimmed with emotion as he added, "You amaze me every day."

Her breath hitched. The moment became almost unbearably intimate, and she felt like he'd laid her bare. It was such a strange thing, having helped a horse give birth, but she could only feel elation at saving two lives at once.

The foal began to nurse after a few more attempts to stand, and Abby watched the pair with her heart expanding more than she'd thought possible.

The vulnerability of the situation, the time of night, Mark's presence—all three things coalesced inside her and made her want to cry. Maybe it was because she felt lonely, or because she would never get to experience giving birth. Which seemed rather silly, comparing herself to a horse, but there it was.

She wiped at her eyes, trying to keep Mark from noticing.

He touched her arm. "What is it?"

She shook her head, but the tears wouldn't stop. They dripped down her face without stopping.

"Abby." He hugged her; this only made the crying worse. Burying her face in his chest, she let herself cry: for herself, for her future. For Mark. For the children she'd never have, for the shame she'd carried.

"Abby," he said again as he rubbed her back. "Talk to me. Aren't you always telling me to talk about things?"

That made her laugh a little. "I can't believe I'm getting this emotional over a horse."

"Tell me about it." His tone was wry enough that it helped her get control of herself.

She wiped her eyes and her nose on her sleeve. She knew she looked terrible, but she was too tired to care. Mark still had his arms around her, which made her feel safer than she'd felt in a long time. When was the last time she'd felt like she could rely on someone else? Not for a while, she realized.

"Did I ever tell you why I broke up with Derek?" she said.

"You said he was an asshole."

That made her smile again. "He was. Still is." She went to sit on the bench again, stretching her legs out in front of her. Mark sat next to her. "When we were dating, though, I found out I have PCOS."

"What is that?"

"Polycystic Ovarian Syndrome. Basically, it means my hormones are all out of sync, and there are lots of different side effects."

Her throat dried up as she considered her next words. She wondered why she was saying anything at all. It was like draining an infection: at first it would hurt, but in the end, it would heal her.

"One of the things that happens is infertility. My doctor

said it would be highly unlikely I'd ever have children. I also have a weirdly shaped uterus. Go figure."

Mark didn't respond, which made Abby antsy. Balling her fists, she waited for him to say something—anything. Even one of the usual useless platitudes. *All things happen for a reason.* Or, *you won't know until you try.* Or, *there are worse things to happen. Be grateful that's all it is.*

"He wanted to end things because of this?" Mark said. "Because you can't have kids?"

Humiliation coursed through her until she was afraid she'd start crying again.

"Basically. I ended things because I knew we were over, but when I told him that, he said no one would want me because I wasn't a real woman."

Mark swore, long and low, and Abby blinked in surprise. His face was flushed, and he looked like he could go on a murderous rampage.

"What a piece of shit," he growled, "to say something like that to you." Cupping her face in his hands, he said, "You are a beautiful, intelligent, amazing woman, Abby Davison. The only reason he said that was because he was pissed that you dared to dump him. Don't you dare believe a word he said."

She covered his hands with hers, hot tears in her eyes. "I think that's the most you've ever said at one time," she said.

He looked a little embarrassed, but she squeezed his wrists. When a tear fell down her cheek, he brushed it away.

"If he were here right now, I'd kill him." Mark kissed her forehead. "Having kids or not having kids doesn't make you less of a person. You're still Abby. Nobody can take that from you."

His words were a balm to her soul, something she hadn't

known she'd needed. She pulled his face down for a deep kiss that made him groan. But right as he was about to pull her close, they heard footsteps.

"Mark? You in there?" An older man stepped into the barn. "How is she?"

"Abby, this is Dr. Walker, the vet." Mark showed Dr. Walker to the stall, where both Delilah and her new foal snoozed.

Abby wanted to go inside to let the men talk, but Mark wouldn't hear of it. He explained to Dr. Walker how Abby had saved the day, and how her quick thinking had saved both Delilah and her foal's lives. Dr. Walker nodded in approval before commending them both.

"Lucky that you had a nurse here. Even if she's a nurse for humans." Dr. Walker winked at her.

The vet gave them both instructions, telling them to watch the foal for any signs that she'd suffered hypoxia, or lack of oxygen due to the placenta detaching too early. He had a feeling she would be fine, considering that she was able to nurse right after she'd been born.

"I'm going to go to sleep," Abby told Mark with a wide yawn as he said goodbye to the vet. "See you inside."

Mark gave her a quick kiss and told her he'd be there soon.

MARK HEARD WATER RUNNING. Elated, exhausted, yet strangely unwilling to go to sleep right now, he went to find Abby.

He needed her with a desire that seemed unquenchable.

The bathroom door was propped open, and he smiled

seeing the cats coming in and out, their tails like question marks. He waited a second, listening for Abby, and he heard her sigh as she stepped into the tub.

He opened the door, his entire body tightening when he saw her nude and glistening.

"Oh!" she said in surprise before laughing a little. "I thought you were one of the cats."

"You always take a bath with company?"

She smiled, her eyes heating as she looked at him. "With feline company, yes. They love running water for some reason. But not usually with human company."

"And what about now?"

She pushed water around, her eyelashes fluttering. "I'd say that if you don't get in this tub with me, then I'll be very disappointed."

Stripping out of his clothes in record speed, he stepped into the tub, which was just large enough for two people. Bubbles covered Abby's breasts, and he groaned when a pink nipple appeared.

He maneuvered her so her back was to him. Kissing and licking the side of her neck, he tasted flowers and salt. Blood rushed to his cock; his pulse beat faster.

Abby arched against him as he cupped her breasts, thumbing her nipples until they were hard little peaks. She'd put her hair in a bun, although tendrils of it had fallen already. She looked like a sultry mermaid, all gleaming curves.

She let out a groan when he nipped her shoulder before soothing the bite with his tongue.

He had the desperate urge to show her that her ex's words were so patently untrue that they were absurd. He'd said them to hurt her, and Mark hated that it seemed to have worked.

Abby had looked so devastated, an expression he never wanted to see on her face again.

He said a grateful prayer that he had both arms and hands to touch her now. One hand kneaded her breast while the other drifted down her body, reveling in the silkiness of her skin.

"How do you always smell so good?" he rumbled. Even after helping to deliver a horse, she still managed to smell good.

She laughed. "Soap is an amazing invention."

He pinched her ass cheek for that remark, which made her squeak. Turning in his arms, she kissed him, licking at his lips and begging for entrance. With her straddling him, her sex pressed against his cock. He could feel her heat, and he swore when she wiggled and arched.

"Keep doing that and this will be over before it even began," he said.

Abby grinned. "Are you saying that if I do this"—she gripped his cock, making his eyes roll back into his head —"that you'll lose control? I can't believe it."

He grunted. Then he swore when she squeezed him and circled her thumb over the tip of his cock.

In revenge, he delved through the petals of her sex, watching as a blush climbed up her cheeks. She continued to stroke him as he rubbed her clit and sank a finger inside her sheath. She bit her bottom lip, but she couldn't stop the sexy little sounds from emerging.

Mark felt her tightening around his fingers. He pulled her closer and kissed her, almost violently, and she shuddered. He pressed her clit with his thumb right as she reached down to fondle his balls. They both moaned, the sounds echoing in the bathroom.

He wanted her to come with his cock inside her, though. He pushed her hands away from his length, gritting his teeth so he didn't completely lose control.

Abby gave him a warm smile as she kissed his sternum, right where his heart beat fast. That organ clenched with an emotion he didn't care to think about. All he would admit was that he needed to be inside her, to feel her tight heat gripping him until he lost himself.

Abby seemed to know what they both needed. Placing her hands on his shoulders for leverage, she sank down onto his cock, taking him inch by excruciating inch. Mark tasted blood from biting his tongue; the feeling of her surrounding him, like a velvet glove, was almost too much. His entire body pulsed; spots raced across his vision.

Abby raised herself up and back down again, taking him in slow strokes. He couldn't help but remember the first time they'd made love, how she'd ridden him like this. He needed more than this—to be not only inside her but over her. Claiming her.

With one arm under her ass and one around her waist, he stepped out of the tub, both of them dripping water onto the floor. He didn't care. Laying her down on the plush rug, he then thrust all the way to the hilt inside her.

"Mark," she cried out. She tilted her head back as he began to move.

She lifted her legs and locked them around his back. With a grunt, he placed his weight on his arms, and although his left arm ached, he didn't care. He only cared about pounding inside Abby until they both lost their minds.

She stroked his face as he rode her, their bodies slapping together. Steam seemed to rise from their very skin, and water droplets landed all over the tile and soaked the rug.

Abby's eyes widened as she began to climax, and Mark drank in her face. Her body arched, the tendons of her neck visible, and when he bit her shoulder, she let out a shout.

Her sheath milked him as she found her release. He gasped and right when his own climax was about to hit, he pulled out of her, coming on her belly.

A few moments later, he barely kept himself from collapsing on top of her. Rolling over, he stared at the ceiling and tried to catch his breath.

Abby finally sat up, letting out a groan. "I think I'm too old to have sex on the floor," she said ruefully.

He laughed. His arm ached and he was exhausted, but looking at Abby, all flushed and replete and beautiful, he didn't care.

"Let's go to bed," he said.

CHAPTER FOURTEEN

Although Abby usually worked days, sometimes she had to work evenings. The day after Delilah gave birth, Abby spent it relaxing and watching the foal tottering around on her long legs. Although Abby and Mark had worried that she might have complications from the difficult birth, as far as they could tell, she was totally healthy.

"I thought you should name her," Mark said that afternoon. The foal nursed with gusto, and based on her already gleaming coat, she'd rival her mother for beauty.

Abby's heart caught in her throat. She had a feeling this was an honor Mark wouldn't bestow on just anyone. Swallowing against the lump in her throat, she replied, "I'll have to think of a good name then."

He put an arm around her waist, kissing her temple. "I know you will."

When Abby arrived at work later that evening, she found Janine in a tizzy. Two other nurses had called in sick with the flu, and now they were short-staffed.

Janine threw her hands up in the air. "And I just got

another kid in here with a broken wrist that needs to be set, and a hysterical mother whose toddler has the croup—"

Abby took the charts that Janine had handed her. "We'll get these all sorted out. How about you go work with the toddler and I'll get this wrist set."

"Pray that we don't get anything else because God knows who will be handling them!"

Abby knew that staying focused, calm, and organized could make or break a shift with as many mishaps as this one. One patient became aggressive when Abby tried to take his blood pressure, while another patient fainted when they had to draw her blood.

Gloria, another RN on staff, arrived to help a few hours into their shift. An older woman with a steady resolve and a sweet bearing, she was exactly what they needed in this chaos.

"Go take a break," she told Abby, seeing how exhausted she was. "You look like you're about to fall over."

It was close to two AM already. Abby yawned, wishing she'd slept in today, but the foal's birth had made sleep impossible. And then making love with Mark afterward...

She shivered at the second memory. She sat down in the break room and drank a hot cup of coffee that tasted like dishwater, but the heat was soothing. Thank God she had tomorrow off.

She needed to think of a name for the foal, didn't she? Getting out her phone, she started to search for suitable names. She wanted something that meant lucky or miraculous. She dismissed a number of choices before she found the perfect one: Mirielle, French for miracle.

She hoped Mark didn't expect her to name the foal something less girly, she thought with a soft laugh. He had told her she could choose whatever name she wanted.

Someone entered the break room. Glancing up from her phone to greet whoever it was, Abby felt the words die in her throat.

It was Derek. Here, at her work, at two in the morning.

He smiled at her, but it was a smile that sent warning bells off in her mind.

She stood up slowly. "Derek? What are you doing here?"

He gestured for her to sit back down. "They told me you were in here, so I decided to come find you. Sit. Let's talk."

She glanced at the clock. "I need to get back to work. You should go home. It's late." As she tried to move past him, he caught her arm, barring her from leaving.

"We need to talk," he said with a hard squeeze on her arm. "*Sit.*"

She considered screaming, but she'd chosen the break room far from the main nurses' station. No one would hear her. *Stupid,* she berated herself.

"How did you find me again?" she asked as she sat down on the edge of a chair.

"One of the nurses said you were on break, and I remembered that you liked this room while we dated. I put two and two together." He shrugged. "I'm glad I caught you. You're a difficult woman to find these days."

She once again glanced at the clock. "I'm more wondering why you're here in the middle of the night."

"When I came in earlier today, they said you had the evening shift. I waited up for you."

Her blood chilled at how easily he'd gotten this information. She needed to have a talk with the staff as soon as possible.

Her main concern, however, was why her ex-boyfriend was so intent on finding her.

"I don't know what you want to talk about." She kept her voice calm and measured.

"Stop playing games, Abby. You already know what I want: I want you."

She dug her fingers into her palms to hide their trembling. "I told you already that that wasn't going to happen. My answer isn't going to change."

A dark look came over his features, but it disappeared in the next instant. "I don't get why you're playing hard to get." He seemed genuinely confused. "This isn't like you."

"I'm not playing anything." She added in a firmer voice, "I'm dating someone else. We're over, Derek."

Derek's cheeks reddened, agitation clear in his expression. He got up to pace.

"We're meant to be together. Why don't you understand that? I should never have let you go." He moved toward her and tried to grab her hand, but she wrenched her arm away.

Standing up, she backed toward the door. "Leave me alone. This is enough. I'm calling security." She reached for the doorknob behind her, but Derek saw her movement before she could open the door.

He wrenched her aside before he slammed and locked the door. The click of the lock sent terror through Abby.

"Why are you doing this?" she whispered.

Derek cornered her, gripping her wrist so hard it hurt. Although he wasn't much bigger than her, he could seriously hurt her if she tried to escape his grasp.

She only hoped she could talk him down, convince him to see reason.

"I want you back," he said, touching her face. She turned away.

He scowled. "I love you, Abby. Don't you get that? I've always loved you. I didn't want us to break up, but you insisted. I've seen how wrong I was to let you go."

He grasped her chin and tried to kiss her, but she slapped him hard enough that he let her go.

Darting behind a chair, she tried to catch her breath. "We're not getting back together. I'm not going to change my mind."

Her fear changed into anger in that moment, disgust lacing her voice. "I'm not in love with you anymore," she said, watching Derek pale. And then, the clincher: "I never loved you in the first place."

Derek stalked toward her. He tried to grab her again, but she snagged a small knife that had been left on the counter.

"Don't touch me," she hissed. "Get out of here before I call the cops and have you arrested." She edged toward the exit, knife in hand.

He rolled his eyes. "You always get so emotional, Abby. Put the knife down. You know you love me; you're just being stubborn."

A red haze covered her vision, and she trembled from sheer rage. Derek had treated her like she was disposable, and his words had haunted her for months. Now he had the gall to act like she'd come running back to him?

"You love me. I know you do," he crooned. "Come on, Abs. Give me the knife."

"Get away from me! I don't love you." She trembled, not

even realizing what she was saying. "I don't love you because I'm in love with Mark."

Everything crystallized in that moment. She couldn't move, and she couldn't speak.

Oh my God, what have I done?

Her words only enraged Derek further. "That guy? What do you even know about him? Just another rich boy who used his parents' money to get where he is. Some loner who nobody likes. Why else would he live by himself out there in the middle of nowhere?" His expression turned into a sneer. "And why would you think he'd ever love somebody like *you*?"

She expected his words to hurt, but this time, they didn't. She was immune to them because Derek didn't have the power to hurt her anymore.

"For your information, he accepts me as I am. He's not a lowlife like you." She smiled a little, remembering how angry Mark's reaction was to her confession. "He's a good man."

Derek was incredulous. "You told him how you can't have kids? That you're only half a woman?"

"I did tell him, although it's none of your business. Like I said, he isn't a jackass like you."

Derek stared at her before he started to move toward her again. Abby raised the knife higher, which only made him smile, his eyes crinkling.

"I wonder if you'd be so brave if I said that I could ruin the man you love."

At her widening eyes, he smiled until his teeth flashed in the fluorescent light. "That got your attention, didn't it? If I can't convince you to come back to me, I can at least prove to you that if you're with anyone else, they'll suffer for it."

Now he got close enough to touch her. He reached out to caress a tendril of hair that had fallen from her ponytail.

Abby was frozen, her fingers hurting from gripping the knife. Derek didn't seem to notice the weapon at all.

"Make your choice, Abby. Know that trying to deny what we have will only end badly for everyone."

Abby waited one more breath before she sliced at his hand with the knife. To her immense satisfaction, blood welled within seconds.

He swore. "You little bitch! I swear to God—"

She unlocked the door and threw it open, running as fast as she could until she reached the nurses' station. She expected Derek to follow her, but when she listened for footsteps, there were none.

Derek had given up—at least for tonight.

She only realized she still held the knife when she reached the nurses' station. With a quick glance around, she was able to stow it away without anyone noticing.

"Whoa, Abby, what the hell? Why are you all red?" Janine asked as she rounded the corner. "Are you all right?"

Abby took a few more deep breaths. "I'm fine. Just getting some exercise." Taking a clipboard from her friend, she asked, "What did I miss?"

"MARK, YOU CAME!" Lizzie exclaimed as she gave him a bear hug. "These two kept saying that you never leave your ranch these days."

Mark hugged his sister before he sat down next to his two older brothers and Heath. They'd come for a few drinks at

The Fainting Goat, the most popular bar in Fair Haven. With Abby at work tonight and Charlie assuring him he'd watch over Delilah and her foal, Mark had accepted his brothers' invitation for a night out.

Besides, being home alone only reminded him how much he missed Abby when she was gone.

I'm turning into such a goddamn sap.

"I only came because Harrison said he'd pay for the first round," Mark said, deadpan.

Lizzie laughed. "Harrison, did you know this?"

Harrison rolled his eyes. "Only until this very moment."

Harrison did, in fact, buy the first round, and Mark noted that Caleb didn't get a beer, but instead some kind of soda. *Interesting.* Since when did Caleb no longer drink? Mark had a feeling it had something to do with Megan Flannigan.

"I haven't been here before," Lizzie said as she looked around the restaurant and bar. She was "dressed to kill," as she'd describe it, wearing tight skinny jeans and a top that showed her toned belly. With her long dark hair and bright red lips, she drew lots of appreciative male gazes.

Lizzie had always been flamboyant, even wild, and she hadn't changed much in that regard. She and Seth had done all kinds of pranks when they'd been younger. Mark remembered one time when the twins had gotten suspended for filling a classroom full of toads. The teacher had continued to find amphibians in her desk drawers days after the clean-up.

Lizzie kept looking around, barely attending to what anyone was saying. Mark, preferring to be silent, watched his little sister.

He wondered why Harrison had chosen this place, or why Lizzie had agreed to come. Everyone knew that Lizzie's ex-boyfriend Trent Younger owned this place. He was often here, checking on his employees and talking to customers.

Lizzie and Trent had had a whirlwind love affair their senior year of high school that had ended almost as abruptly as it had begun. Mark didn't know the details of their breakup, but right after they'd ended things, Lizzie had run off with her band, avoiding Fair Haven—and Trent—for years.

Right now, Lizzie couldn't sit still; her anxiety made Mark anxious from watching her.

"Liz, where were you last touring?" Caleb asked her. "Was it San Francisco?"

Lizzie blinked, confused. "What? Sorry, I was thinking about something."

"Or someone," Mark muttered, but Harrison kicked him under the table.

"Where were you last on your tour?" Heath offered.

Heath was all kindness compared to the rough-and-tumble Thornton brothers. Working with elementary-school students gave him more patience than most people. Smiling at Lizzie, he waited for her response.

Mark narrowed his eyes at Heath. He'd seen how he'd looked at Jubilee on Thanksgiving.

That guy better watch himself.

Lizzie smiled. "Oh, yeah. It was LA. I was also there to record my next album. It's crazy to think that I have more than one album, you know?"

"It's crazy to think my baby sister is some celebrity musician," Harrison said. He tugged on her hair. "I remember you as the girl who put worms in my bed."

That made her laugh. "Was that you? I thought it was Caleb."

"It was both of us," Caleb said wryly.

The last time Mark had heard his sister perform, she'd blown him away with her talent. He was no musician, but even he could recognize skill when he heard it.

She'd played with a mixture of pure emotion and technical skill, her lyrics as beautiful as the notes she strummed on her guitar. Mark wasn't surprised that she'd been as successful as she'd been.

"Oh my God, is that—? Lizzie Thornton?" Two girls approached their table, eyes wide.

"It is you! I knew you were from here, but you haven't been around in so long," the other girl gushed.

Lizzie grinned. "I'm here now. How are you?"

After a brief conversation, the girls left with autographs in hand.

Lizzie turned back to the guys, who were staring at her. "What?" she demanded.

"Well, we never thought about you being famous," Caleb said with a shake of his head. "It's weird."

"It is weird," Mark confirmed.

"You guys are weird. And I think it's time for another drink." Lizzie motioned to a waitress.

As the evening passed, Lizzie kept drinking. Her cheeks became flushed, and she kept laughing too loudly at every little thing.

"I think you've had enough," Caleb said when she tried to order another drink.

She scowled. "I'm fine. Stop being annoying." She began to fall over, Heath catching her. She laughed.

The three brothers looked at each other. Before they could make a decision, Mark saw the last person Lizzie needed to see right now: Trent Younger.

Trent was tall with blond hair, tattoos circling his arms and neck. As far as Mark knew, Trent hadn't had a serious relationship since he'd dated Lizzie, preferring to keep things casual. He didn't lack for bedmates, that was for certain, especially as he opened more restaurants that only increased his wealth and notoriety.

But right now, he only had eyes for Lizzie. Lizzie didn't notice him at first, and Mark hoped they could get her out of here before she saw him.

But it was like they had some invisible connection, because within a moment, Lizzie turned, meeting Trent's gaze from across the room.

Mark heard her inhale.

The pair stared at each other; nobody said a word. Although the restaurant bustled with activity, you could've heard a pin drop in the silence.

Trent's expression shuttered before he walked to their table.

"Goddammit," Harrison muttered. He tipped back the rest of his drink. "Here we go."

Lizzie turned away when Trent arrived.

"How's everything here? Nice to see you guys." His gaze flickered over Lizzie for a brief moment.

Lizzie ignored him, drawing circles on the table.

"Hey Trent," Caleb said. "How's it been?"

"Good. Busy. You?" He looked at Harrison. "I hear congrats are in order?"

"That's right. You're invited to the wedding, you know."

Trent smiled, but it didn't reach his eyes. "Good, otherwise I was going to crash it."

The guys talked for a while longer, updating each other about their lives. Lizzie continued to ignore Trent until the tension became so thick Mark felt himself growing tense.

Finally, Trent said, "Lizzie. It's been a long time."

"Hi." She still wouldn't look at him.

"I heard your band is doing well. Congratulations."

Now she looked at him from the corner of her eye. "Thanks. Congrats to you too. This place is great."

Trent clenched his jaw. Nobody spoke. Mark wished he could get another beer to forget any of this had happened.

"I thought maybe we could get a drink some time," Trent said in a low voice. "To catch up."

She finally turned to face him. "Why would I want to do that? No, I'm good. I won't be in town for long anyway." Sliding off her seat, she stumbled. Trent caught her.

"I'll take Lizzie home," Caleb said as he tossed a few dollars onto the table. "See you guys, later."

He took Lizzie's elbow, although Trent seemed reluctant to let her go. He said something to Lizzie and finally stalked away.

"What was that all about?" Heath asked, gesturing over his shoulder.

Mark and Harrison looked at each other. Then they both shrugged. "Don't even ask, man," Harrison replied. "You don't want to know."

"He means that we don't actually know the answer," Mark added.

Harrison grunted. "That, too."

As Mark got into his truck after saying goodbye to

Harrison and Heath, he sat in the driver's seat and stared out at nothing. Seeing Lizzie and Trent at odds like that made him wonder if he was going to end up in the same situation with Abby. Those two had been in love once, and neither had seemed to move on.

So why couldn't they make it work?

Mark knew he'd closed himself off from the world after Tina had cheated on him, and for what? To keep himself safe? That was no kind of life. He'd been a coward not to tell Abby the truth about Tina's betrayal, about how his best friend had betrayed him, too.

He closed his eyes as old wounds resurfaced.

How could he let himself love again when the possibility terrified him to his very marrow?

CHAPTER FIFTEEN

Mark was awake when he heard Abby return from work around seven AM. Yawning and stretching, he rose from the bed, a smile tugging at his lips when he saw the two cats curled up at the end of his bed.

He'd tossed and turned for hours after getting home last night. He'd wanted to tell Abby everything about Tina, and yet the last thing he wanted was her pity. His pride had forbidden him from talking about how the woman he'd once loved had betrayed him with another man. So why the sudden need to confess all?

What did it say about Mark himself, that his former girlfriend had thrown him over for his best friend? He wondered sometimes if he hadn't caused Tina to stray. If he'd paid more attention to her, if he'd told her how much he'd loved her, if he'd been charming and funny and everything Aaron had been, maybe things would've been different.

He wondered if he could expect love from any woman when he felt like he was damaged goods.

He heard Abby go to her room. He went to the kitchen to

wait for her, but when she didn't show even for a cup of coffee, concern filled him. Perhaps she was so tired that she'd gone straight to bed, he reasoned, but something itched in the back of his mind.

"Abby?" he murmured as he knocked on her door. To his surprise, it was shut completely, so not even the cats could get in. The two felines were already meowing at the door and turning in circles. He tried the handle, but it was locked.

"Abby? Open up. Are you okay?"

He was seriously considering breaking down the door when she finally opened it. He took in her red eyes and her wet cheeks, his concern increasing.

"What is it? What happened?"

He tried to touch her, embrace her, but she pulled away. He watched in confusion as she sat on her bed and started crying.

He didn't know what to do. She wouldn't talk to him, and her crying scared him. Kneeling in front of her, he took her hands from her face and squeezed her fingers.

"Please tell me what's wrong. Please. Abby, you're killing me."

She wiped her eyes on her shoulder, sniffling and hiccupping. "I was so scared. I've never been so scared." Her voice hitched.

"Scared of what, baby? Tell me."

Her eyes widened a little at the endearment. "Derek came to my work this morning. He...threatened me."

Mark's vision went black for a moment. He had to let go of her hands so he didn't crush them. It was only seeing Abby's tearstained face that kept him from losing control.

"Tell me what happened," he said as he sat next to her.

She told him, at first in halting sentences, and then in surer tones. By the time she'd finished, she wasn't shaking from fear—it was from a rage mirrored by Mark himself.

He got up and started to pace, fists clenching and unclenching. He thought of how it would feel to punch that asshole in the face, and then keep punching him until he cried for mercy. He'd make him beg for him to stop.

"Did you call the cops?" Mark asked her.

She shook her head. "I just wanted to get out of there. I know. It was stupid." Her voice seemed choked. "I wanted to get back here. To you. I wanted to finish my shift and drive here until I felt safe again."

His rage dissipated, a different emotion taking hold of his heart. Wrapping an arm around her, he held her close, wishing he could erase her fear completely.

"I'm going to get a restraining order today, though," Abby said. "Or at least apply for one. However that works."

"Caleb can help. If all else fails, I'll make him your bodyguard."

That made her smile. "You won't be my bodyguard?"

"No, because I'll be too busy tracking that piece of shit down and making him pay." He snarled the words.

She stiffened. "Don't go after him. Please. If anything should happen to you..."

"Nothing will happen to me."

"You don't know that." She took his face in her hands. "Please, Mark. Don't do anything. If you were hurt or worse —" She swallowed, pressing against him.

He finally said, "Then you need to stay here where I can look out for you. Don't leave yet."

She didn't say anything, but merely sighed.

He made her look up at him.

"Stay with me, Abby. I'll keep you safe."

Her eyes filled with some emotion he couldn't identify. She nodded. "I'll stay."

He kissed her forehead, and then he kissed her nose and then her cheeks, tasting the salt of her tears. She whispered his name when he kissed her mouth, the kiss deepening within moments. Lust coursed through Mark's veins, and he ran a hand down her back. She moaned, arching, her breath increasing.

He wanted to topple her onto her bed and screw her senseless until they were both exhausted, but something told him not to. Not now. Not yet. She was vulnerable, she needed to rest—

He ended the kiss, but he didn't let her go. "You should sleep," he said when she looked confused.

"Then stay with me? I don't want to be alone right now."

He had things to do but right now? None of it mattered. After pulling down the covers, he held her in his arms and waited for her to fall asleep.

ABBY AWOKE to the sun shining through her window. Yawning, she saw that Mark had left already, although the bed was still warm where he'd lain with her. Her heart filled.

She found him outside with Delilah and her foal. The foal was already trotting around the enclosure, which made her smile for the first time today. Abby folded her arms on top of the fence and watched.

Mark laughed when Delilah nudged his shoulder, and he

turned to rub her nose. The foal decided she didn't like to be ignored and tried to nip his jacket. Before Mark could react, the foal dodged away, playing like a child.

Abby entered the enclosure and said, "I figured out a name for her."

"Really?" Mark leaned against the fence and watched the horses. Rosemary grazed on a remaining patch of green grass, while Samson cantered around, snorting when the foal got too close.

"I thought you should name her Mirielle." At his raised eyebrow, she explained, "It means 'miracle.'"

"Ah. Mirielle." His lips quirked upward. "I like it. It suits her. Although I'm not sure she's so much a miracle as lucky that you were there in the first place."

Mirielle nudged her mother, stopping to nurse. Delilah's tail swished back and forth, not at all aware of how close her baby had come to death's door.

"I called Caleb while you slept," Mark said quietly, still watching the horses. "He said that you definitely have a case to get a restraining order and that he'll help you in any way he can."

Her mood dampened at the mention of Derek. She sighed and rubbed her temples. "He wasn't this bad when we were dating. I don't know what's happened to him."

"Some men react badly to rejection." As he turned his gaze toward her, he said, "I know I'd feel the same, if you told me we were over."

Her heart clenched. "Mark..."

"I know. I mean, we were never real to begin with." He dragged his fingers through his hair, disheveling the locks. "But do you think we could try? To have something real? And not just an affair, like you called it. Something else." He looked uncomfortable then, and he hooked his fingers in his back pockets, no longer looking her in the eye.

But now she smiled so widely that her cheeks hurt. This impossible, gruff, ridiculous man would be the end of her, but in the best possible way.

"Yes, I would like that. Very much."

She felt the words bubbling up inside, the big *L* word wanting to break through the surface, but she couldn't find the courage to say it. Not yet.

Although Mark was not as closed-off as he had been even a few weeks ago, she still sensed a distance in him. She didn't know if she could ever overcome the walls he'd placed around his heart.

How could you convince a man who thought love only hurt you that your love was different?

He smiled then, and his handsomeness took her breath away. He kissed her, so sweetly that she was afraid she'd burst into tears. She didn't know if she were happier that he'd asked her to make this more than an affair, or if she were more afraid that this was as far as they'd ever get.

CHAPTER SIXTEEN

After a long day at the local courthouse to obtain a restraining order, Abby left with a temporary order in hand. Her heart felt a little lighter, although both she and Mark knew that a restraining order was just a piece of paper. It helped, but it wasn't going to stop Derek if he wanted to hurt Abby, unfortunately.

Caleb had told them he would do everything in his power as a police officer to assist her. Based on the evidence provided and with Caleb's help, the judge had agreed to issue an immediate restraining order. The court would notify Derek, and another hearing would be held at a later date.

Abby was quiet as she walked with Mark back to his truck. This hadn't been what she'd imagined doing on her day off. She got spooked by random noises, afraid that it was Derek returning to finish what he'd started.

Sometimes she had a hard time believing he would hurt her—at least physically. Hurt her with words? Absolutely. But he'd never threatened her like this when they'd been dating.

"Let's go get something to eat," Mark said. "I'll pay."

She wasn't hungry, but she shrugged and followed him to a diner a block away from the courthouse. A greasy spoon, it smelled like burgers and cheese, and for some reason, Abby found it comforting.

Mark ordered a burger and fries. Abby stared at the menu, the words like a foreign language. She should order something. She hadn't eaten since last night.

"I'll have a milkshake," she said finally.

"That's all?" Mark asked her as the waitress walked away.

"I'm not hungry."

He gave her a concerned look. She felt oddly embarrassed, for some reason. She knew it was a strange emotion to associate with this situation. Her vulnerability embarrassed her, she realized. That she'd had to take legal action against a man she'd once believed she'd loved—a man she'd thought had loved *her*!

How had she been so blind to miss the warning signs? She'd seen enough domestic violence cases as a nurse that she'd always assumed she'd know better. It reminded her that anyone could become a victim of something like domestic violence—even somebody like her.

Their food arrived soon after, and Abby sipped at her milkshake, lost in thought. Mark was silent. Abby was too exhausted to care how awkward this lunch date had become.

"Abby," Mark said.

She looked up from her milkshake.

"Are you okay? You're never this quiet."

That made her smile a little. "I'm just really tired. I want this to all be over."

"I know. But I'll keep you safe—you have my promise."

That made her want to cry. She could only nod, drinking

the rest of her milkshake even though it had become like a lead weight in her stomach.

Later outside, Abby almost ran into Mark's back as he stopped in his tracks. She moved around him to see what he was looking at.

Or more accurately, *who* he was looking at.

It was a couple: a pretty—and very pregnant woman—and her husband had come out of a store across the street. They seemed innocuous enough, although the woman's dress was a very flamboyant shade of pink that made her look like a gum ball.

"Mark?" Abby touched his arm. "Mark? Now you're freaking me out."

He glanced down at her. "What? Sorry. It's nothing."

He guided her back toward his truck, and he began to walk so quickly that Abby almost had to run to keep up.

"Mark!" A voice called out.

Abby turned to see the couple approaching them, and Abby saw that the woman was beautiful, almost in an ethereal kind of way. But it wasn't just that she was beautiful: she was the woman from the photograph. The recognition hit Abby square in the chest.

This was Tina, Mark's ex. The ex who'd cheated on him and broken his heart.

Her breath whooshed from her chest. Was this man the one she'd slept with while dating Mark? Abby had to restrain her own surge of anger at the thought.

What kind of person betrayed someone she claimed to love? How could she do that to Mark, a man whose heart was worth more than this woman could imagine?

"I'm so glad we ran into you again," Tina said. Her gaze flicked toward Abby. "I don't believe we've met...?"

Mark scowled, not replying.

"I'm Abby Davison." Abby reached out a hand, although she struggled with how she should introduce herself. As a friend? Girlfriend? Her head hurt.

"She's my girlfriend," Mark interjected, answering the question for her. "This is Tina and her husband Aaron. We used to be friends."

Tina flinched, although her expression was sad. Guilty. Abby wanted to crawl into a hole out of secondhand embarrassment.

Tina and Aaron looked both upset and contrite, while Mark looked angry. And Abby didn't want to see any of this because it was none of her business, because at the end of the day, who was she to Mark? He sort-of girlfriend? The woman he'd made a deal with weeks ago?

"I'm going back to the truck," she said, but Mark kept hold of her hand.

"No, I want you to meet these two." He gestured at them both. "Did I tell you the entire story? No? It's actually pretty funny."

Abby tried to leave, but Mark held firm. She had a feeling he'd forgotten all about her.

"Tina was my girlfriend, and Aaron here, he was my best friend." Mark smiled grimly.

Glancing at Tina and Aaron, who looked stricken, she wished she was anywhere else but here right now.

"I thought I'd fallen in love with Tina. I even bought her a ring."

Tina covered her mouth in surprise.

"I never told you that, did I?" His expression turned into a sneer, and it sent a frisson of fear through Abby's heart. "I had the ring in my pocket when I came back to our house and found her and Aaron screwing like rabbits. In my bed."

Abby winced. There it was, then. Abby had guessed correctly, and she hated that she'd been right. Her heart ached for Mark, and her heart even ached for the pair standing in front of them, standing frozen and horrified.

"I threw Aaron out of my house and beat the shit out of him, and then I told Tina to get out. I tossed the ring into the nearest lake. And now look at them. Married, going to have a baby, like nothing ever happened."

"Mark..." Abby dug her nails into his arm. "Let's go. This isn't going to help anything."

"If you're going to blame anyone, blame me," Aaron said. His voice was hoarse. "I loved Tina since that first day I met her. I tried to stay away from her, but it just...happened."

Mark laughed, but nobody else did. "So someone else took off your pants and had sex with my girlfriend in my bed?"

"Mark, please." Tina's bottom lip trembled. "I'm sorry. We both are. We can't ever begin to make up for what we did."

When Tina instinctively covered her pregnant belly with her hand, Abby saw Mark visibly deflate. Right then, he looked tired and almost dead inside.

He muttered, "You can't make up for what you did. It's not something you can forgive someone for."

And in the next moment, Mark stalked away, leaving Abby behind.

She wanted to say something to the pair, but at the same time, wasn't Mark's anger valid? They'd almost destroyed him, and she could only imagine the pain of seeing these two married and expecting a child, while he'd been left behind. Forgotten.

"How could you do that to him?" she whispered, surprised she'd said the words to these strangers. "How could you?"

"It wasn't—it just happened." Tina's voice was pleading. "We didn't plan on it happening."

"Does it matter? Just because you didn't plan on stepping on my foot doesn't mean it doesn't hurt me." Abby shook her head. "If you're looking for absolution from the man you wronged, it's not going to happen. Either accept what you did or don't."

Abby saw Aaron wrap his arm around Tina before she turned to follow Mark.

Abby rested her hand on Mark's back before he got into his truck. She felt his heart thumping, felt the rise and fall of his trembling breaths. Felt how hot his body was through the fabric of his shirt. And she felt his pain like it was her own.

"We should go," he muttered, but he didn't move.

Abby leaned against him, resting her cheek on his back. She couldn't find any words, because what words would make this right? There were none.

Mark swore under his breath, long and low, before turning around and wrapping his arms around her. He hugged her so hard that she almost couldn't breathe, but she didn't break the embrace. He shook in her arms. Her heart broke a million times over.

"I'm sorry," she whispered. She heard people walking past, heard voices, but it didn't matter. She didn't care if everyone stared at them.

"It's not your fault."

"Doesn't mean the sentiment isn't still meant."

He let out a breath and finally, he let her go. He didn't say another word as he got into his truck. Abby went to the other side and got in, but he didn't turn on the engine. Gripping the steering wheel, he gazed at something in the distance, unseeing, unhearing.

"Do you know what the worst part is?" he said hoarsely. He still didn't look at her, but his hands clenched on the steering wheel. "The worst is that they've moved on and I haven't."

Abby swallowed her tears. She was tired and heartsick and she wished she had some way to heal Mark's hurt, but she was at a loss.

"They moved on, got married, and are having a baby like nothing happened. Where's the justice in that?" His voice rose, his fingers white from gripping the steering wheel. "How do they get to live their lives as if they did nothing wrong? And here I am, doing what?" He scoffed, disgust lacing his tone. "Living like some monk on a ranch, proving that she made the right choice in dumping me for Aaron."

She hated hearing this from him. Part of her wanted to hug him again, while the other part wanted to shake him until his teeth rattled.

"They may have moved on in a way, but if you'd really seen their faces..." She smiled grimly. "To say this haunts them would be an understatement."

"Good. I hope it makes their lives hell." And then in another breath, he leaned his forehead against the steering wheel, took a deep breath, and then looked over at Abby with sad eyes.

"I'm sorry you had to see that. Or hear me complaining." He ran his fingers through his hair. "Jesus, I sound so pathetic.

You shouldn't have to hear me whine about shit like this. I need to get it fucking together."

"I want to hear it." Her heart pounded as the words rose in her throat, but this time, they weren't out of fear. They were out of a need for honesty.

"I want to hear it because I love you. I love *you*, Mark. All of you—even the pathetic parts."

He stared at her, completely stunned. He turned as white as a sheet, his mouth opening and closing. Words seemed out of reach for him for a moment.

As time stretched until it was so tense that Abby almost trembled, she forced herself to wait. Even if her courage was crumbling with every passing second.

Then: "Jesus, Abby, you *can't*."

Her chin wobbled. "I can't love you? Why? Is it such an impossible thing?"

"I don't deserve that. Not from you."

Her anger flared. "Don't you dare. Don't you dare put me on some kind of pedestal like a saint. I'm not."

"If you're not a saint, then what does that make me?" He laughed, that same laugh that had sent chills down Abby's spine. "I can't believe this."

"What's so hard to believe? Do you think I'm lying?" Her anger rose along with her voice. "Am I so unlovable?"

That got his attention. "No—no. Jesus Christ. *No*. You are —" He swallowed, licked his lips. "You're everything," he whispered. "You have to know that, Abby."

Now the tears wouldn't stop. "Then why?"

"Because love isn't for me. Love is something that hurts you in the end. I stopped believing in it a long time ago." He looked off into the distance again. "I'm not the guy who can give you that. I'm sorry."

Now it was her turn to laugh. It startled Mark enough that he gaped at her.

"You're sorry? I don't want your pity, Mark Thornton." She pointed a finger at him. "You're only saying this because you've kept yourself away from people ever since Tina hurt you. I don't know how anyone could get over the walls around your heart. You want to talk about being sorry for someone? I feel sorry for you. You'd rather stay in your castle, alone forever, then take a step outside and risk getting hurt when there could be something life-changing on the other side."

His expression was stark. They stared at each other in silence, as if they could bend the other by sheer force of will.

"I love you, Mark Thornton," Abby murmured, "but I refuse to have my heart broken by you out of fear."

He inhaled. "What does that mean?"

"It means we're over. I'm going home, where I belong." She wiped her eyes and stiffened her spine. "Although I'll need to get my things. And my cats. So we better head out."

"Who will keep you safe? I'm not going to let you go home and be alone right now."

She knew he was right: she should stay at the ranch. It was safer. The restraining order felt heavy in her pocket.

"I'll risk it." She curled her hands into fists, feeling the bite of her nails in her palms. "Because in all honesty, being near you right now hurts worse than anything Derek could do to me."

He didn't say anything. Instead, Abby could feel the walls going up, and she knew she couldn't climb over them. Not unless he took a bulldozer to them himself.

Two hours later she arrived home, Darcy and Wentworth meowing pitifully from their carrier. It was only until she collapsed onto her bed that she let herself cry.

She cried so hard that the cats came to snuggle against her, her tears only drying up when she fell into an exhausted sleep.

CHAPTER SEVENTEEN

"We'll be fine. Seriously." Abby tried not to sound exasperated, but she couldn't stand it when people hovered.

"You're sure?" Megan pressed.

Caleb stood behind Megan. After Abby had arrived at her apartment, she hadn't been home longer than a few hours when Megan had come knocking. "Mark called us," she'd explained. "He wanted you to stay with me and Caleb for now just to be safe."

Although the last thing Abby had wanted was to be around other people—and especially Mark's brother—she'd agreed because it was a wise thing to do. Megan had assured her that she'd come by to see to the cats while Abby was at work.

Now, though, Caleb and Megan were about to skip out on their date because of her.

"My mom will be here, and you're just a phone call away," Abby assured them. She started to push them out the door.

This made Megan laugh. "Fine! Fine! We'll leave you alone."

"I'll have my radio with me," Caleb said. "And you have Gonzalez's number, right?"

Officer Gonzalez was Caleb's boss at the police station. Abby sighed. "Yes, I have his number. Now, go before I kick you out. Literally."

Abby shut the door with another sigh.

It had been a week since she'd last seen Mark. A week since she'd talked to him, or kissed him, or had told him that she loved him.

She'd already cried more than enough times. She'd cried until her head had ached, and she'd been a red, stuffy mess. Megan had made Abby take a hot bath when she'd arrived before Megan had tucked her into bed like a child.

Megan knew better than most how these Thornton men could break your heart. "They're kind of too good at it," she'd admitted. "Caleb just about broke me, the idiot. My only consolation was that I think he fell apart even more than I did."

There was some small consolation in Mark suffering, Abby had to admit. But then the thought of him hurting made *her* hurt, and she cursed him for the millionth time for being so cowardly and stubborn.

Fiona arrived some fifteen minutes later. She hadn't been able to get off work until now, although Abby had told her some of what had happened already. She gave Abby a huge hug, which only made Abby want to cry again.

Apparently she wasn't out of tears like she'd thought.

"Come on. We're going to eat takeout and you're going to

tell your mom everything," Fiona said in a brisk voice as she hustled Abby inside.

Abby told her the entire story, starting with the initial lie that she'd told Fiona two months ago. Although Fiona looked like she wanted to interject, she kept her mouth shut as the words spilled out.

Abby told her about moving to Mark's ranch, how he'd told her she could leave whenever she wanted soon thereafter. About how he'd accepted her, infertility and all. Then the foal, Derek, everything. When she finally stopped talking, both she and Fiona were crying.

"Abby, this is all my fault," her mom said through her tears. She grabbed a tissue, dabbing at her eyes. "I should never have tried to interfere like I did. I just want you to be happy. I know how broken-hearted you were after you broke up with Derek."

"Don't blame yourself. Don't. I should never have lied. I should never have agreed to Mark's terms." Abby shook her head. "I think, even though I was angry that he tried to black-mail me, I was intrigued by him enough to want to say yes. How screwed up is that?"

"As screwed up as a mother forcing her daughter into this situation to begin with?" Fiona sniffled and blew her nose.

"This is definitely not your fault. Derek would've tried something regardless." Abby leaned her head against the back of the couch. "What am I going to do?" she whispered. "I still love Mark, even if I want to strangle him."

Fiona considered. A still-handsome woman in her late fifties, she had been Abby's mother as well as her confidante. Although Abby hadn't liked Fiona setting her up on terrible blind dates, she'd understood the impulse behind them.

Fiona had been alone ever since Abby's father had died when Abby had been small; she'd never wanted to remarry. But Abby sometimes wondered if she hadn't remarried because she'd been too dedicated to raising Abby.

Fiona knew all too well what it was like to be alone, and Abby knew she'd been trying to help, in her own way.

"Do you believe he loves you?" Fiona asked.

Abby chewed on her lip. "I don't know. He's so closed-off. I don't know how I can reach him, you know? He has these walls around himself."

"True, but do you know what I think?"

"What?"

"A man who didn't love you wouldn't have cared about your safety after you left. He wouldn't have called his older brother and told him to watch over you when he couldn't." Fiona leaned forward and took Abby's hand, squeezing it. "A man who didn't love you wouldn't have let you name his beloved new foal, and he wouldn't have told you his darkest secrets."

"Then why did he say those things to me? Why tell me that I shouldn't love him?"

"You already said it yourself: he's afraid. He had his heart broken once. And I can tell you right now, the thought of *you* breaking his heart? It's so terrifying that he'd rather push you away."

Abby drank in her mother's words, like a balm to her soul. She wanted to believe it all; she wanted to believe that Mark loved her, despite everything.

But she couldn't force a man to love her, could she?

After they ate their takeout, Abby leaned her head on

Fiona's shoulder, her eyelids heavy. Fiona stroked her hair like she used to do when Abby was little.

"Tell me it'll be all right," Abby murmured.

Fiona kissed the top of her head. "It'll be all right, sweetheart."

~

MARK WATCHED Delilah and Mirielle canter about the enclosure. Although he loved to see the foal flourish with every passing day, it wasn't enough to heal the remnants of his tattered heart.

Without Abby, life was meaningless. Food tasted like ash; the sun was dimmer, the world lacking in color. If he were a writer, he'd be writing page after page of maudlin, syrupy poetry about Abby's eyes. Her hair. Her laugh.

Her love.

He didn't deserve her love, but he ached for it. He wanted it more than he'd wanted anything else on this earth.

And with that realization came the even more obvious one: he loved her.

He loved her so much he couldn't draw breath for wanting her back at his side.

But he knew it was over. He'd let her go, because she should live a life without him holding her back. He was damaged goods—everyone knew that. Abby had seen it for herself that day when they'd run into Tina and Aaron.

"You have visitors," Charlie said as he stopped by the fence to watch the horses.

It took Mark a second to register Charlie's words. "Who?"

"It's us, your favorite brothers," Caleb announced. He and Harrison approached, nodding at Charlie.

"Oh, it's you guys." Mark looked away, but not before adding, "Charlie, these are my brothers. Have you met them? They weren't invited, by the way."

"Nice to meet you, Charlie. I'm glad Mark is back to his old hospitable self," Harrison said as he shook Charlie's hand.

"How do you work with this guy?" Caleb shook his head as he took Charlie's hand in a friendly clasp.

"Beats me. I just keep my mouth shut." Charlie shrugged as he returned to the barn.

Mark didn't know why his brothers were here. Actually, that was a lie. They were probably here to lecture him about something, and he wasn't in the mood for their bullshit.

"Is that your new foal?" Caleb asked. "What's her name again?"

"Mirielle." The name reminded him of Abby, which made his heart hurt.

"She's beautiful. I can see why you're so attached to them," Harrison said.

Mark wanted to tell them about how Abby had saved both Delilah and Mirielle, but the words were stuck in his throat. He couldn't talk about Abby because it hurt too damn much.

"So you're probably wondering why we're here," Caleb ventured as he leaned his forearms on the fence.

Mirielle shook her head right then, kicking up dust as she tried to chase her mother. Rosemary made sure to get out of the way, while Samson decided he'd try to race the foal.

"I think I can guess," Mark replied.

After he'd dropped Abby off at her house, he'd called Caleb right away. Mark hadn't explained everything that had happened, but he'd gotten Caleb to agree to let Abby stay with him and Megan. Caleb had told Mark he'd get the whole story out of him one way or another.

"I know you won't ask, but Abby's doing okay. Not great, though. She's sad, and she won't even talk to Megan." Caleb raised a dark eyebrow. "And now Megan is annoyed with me because I'm related to you. So, I blame you twice over for me not getting any last night."

Mark rubbed at his chest. "Abby and I are over. There's nothing else to talk about."

At that, Harrison snorted. Crossing his arms, he said, "You look about as over her as I did when Sara told me things were over between us. Guess what? She was wrong, and I decided that nothing was going to stop me from getting her back."

"So that's it, then? You decide it's over and you're going to let her go?" Caleb rolled his eyes. "Dude, she's in love with you, and unless I'm missing the obvious, you're in love with her, too. What's holding you back?"

Mark had never told his brothers what had happened with Tina. All they knew was that they'd broken up after dating for a few years.

But right then, the burden felt so heavy that he couldn't carry it all inside anymore.

In a halting voice laced with anger and humiliation, he recounted the story, hoping this would be the last time he had to tell it.

His brothers were silent. Mark didn't know how they'd react. With pity? Disgust? Judgment that Mark was still angry about it?

Then, Harrison said: "I'm sorry that happened. Really."

"But if you let Abby go because those two assholes

screwed you over, then you know what you're doing?" Caleb gave him a pointed look. "You're letting them win. And God knows you don't want that to be true."

Mark's voice was rough as he said, "It's not that simple."

"What's not that simple? Telling Abby that you love her, that you're sorry for being an idiot, and that you want her back," Harrison said. "You might need to grovel—"

"—Majorly grovel," Caleb interjected.

"But if she really loves you, then at least you have a chance." His voice lower, Harrison said, "Don't close yourself off forever, Mark. That's no way to live life."

"Even though Harrison says a lot of bullshit, he's right." Caleb smiled. "Being stuck in the past so much that it destroys your future is no way to live."

Harrison thumped Mark on the shoulder. "You're worthy of way more than you think."

Mark glanced at his eldest brother, surprised, and he saw Harrison look away in embarrassment. Mark's mouth twisted in a semblance of a smile.

The three brothers watched the horses in silence for some time, no longer needing to say anything. After a time, Charlie returned to lead the horses back into the barn for their evening feeding.

To his surprise, Mark felt a sense of peace for the first time.

Even though he didn't want to admit it, his brothers were right. If he stayed where he was, he'd let what Tina and Aaron did control his life. And in the process, he'd lose Abby —the woman he loved more than life itself.

Caleb cleared his throat. "I feel like I need to do something really manly now. Like chop wood. Throw logs into a lake. Wear flannel. You know, manly things."

"Why the hell would you throw logs into a lake?" Harrison countered. "That's a total waste of chopped wood."

"It was just an example! Screw you guys, I'm going to go do something so manly I'll grow an entire pelt of chest hair in the process."

But Caleb laughed, and Mark told him he'd chop off his hand if he tried to chop wood. This meant Harrison, Caleb and Mark had to decide how to do a wood-chopping battle to prove who was, in fact, the manliest.

Their banter was cut short when the acrid scent of smoke filled the air.

"Is there a bonfire somewhere?" Caleb asked, looking around. "Or someone burning leaves?"

Mark froze. This wasn't the scent of burning leaves or of a bonfire.

His turned to see smoke and flames rising from the barn, where both Charlie and the horses were now trapped inside.

CHAPTER EIGHTEEN

After finishing her shift for the day, Abby had stopped by her place to feed Darcy and Wentworth before driving to Mark's. Her heart-to-heart with Fiona had shown her that she couldn't let Mark run from her.

If he truly loved her—which she hoped and prayed was true—then why should things end like this?

Her phone rang as she drove, and she didn't even look at the caller ID when she answered. "Hello?"

"Abby?"

Her breath caught when she heard the voice—not Mark, like she'd hoped.

It was Derek.

She was about to disconnect the call when Derek said, "If you hang up, your boyfriend is going to pay for it."

She gritted her teeth. "You have a lot of nerve to call me when you know I have a restraining order against you. What the hell do you want?"

"I don't want anything. I mean, I do, but I wanted you to

know that I'm *here*." He let out a nervous laugh, and Abby heard some kind rustling.

"What are you doing, Derek?" she said very slowly. "Is this worth getting yourself arrested? Put in jail for the rest of your life?"

"It doesn't matter anymore. You told me you didn't want me, so I'm going to destroy what you wanted." His tone was almost bland, like he were talking about going to the grocery store.

It only made Abby more terrified.

"But if you do come back to me," he added, "I won't burn this ranch to the ground."

"No, Derek, you wouldn't. Don't." Abby struggled to find the words to convince him to stop whatever he'd planned. Pushing on the gas, she drove as fast as she could, hoping she could keep Derek on the phone long enough to arrive in time.

How did you convince a madman to do something sane, though?

"I know I wasn't good enough to you. I should've made you stay. I should never have told you weren't woman enough because that just made you mad." Derek sounded almost mournful. "I know you hate me now, but if I could prove to you that I love you more than anything... Doesn't that mean anything, Abby? Doesn't my love count for something?"

She took a deep breath, forced herself to stay calm. Inwardly, she was shaking, and she didn't know how she managed to speak and continue to drive. Her nurse's brain reasoned that she was probably in shock.

"Sometimes things don't work out how we'd like them to," she said, almost gently. "Sometimes one person loves somebody who doesn't love them back. Sometimes love doesn't last. It's just life."

"Because you think this Thornton guy would love you more than I would? Except I heard around town that you returned home because he'd dumped you. Weird, huh?"

"You don't know what you're talking about."

"Don't I? Well, if you don't care about him, then what I do next won't matter, will it?"

She could hear the shrug in his voice. In the distance, she could see Mark's ranch, and she prayed harder than she'd prayed before that she'd get there in time.

"Don't do this. It's not worth it." She let out a sad laugh. "I'm not worth it. You'll find somebody else."

Derek let out a little screech. "I don't want anyone else! It's you, Abby. It's *you!*"

Then there was a thump, and Abby wasn't sure what had happened. "Derek? Derek! What are you doing?"

"This." He requested FaceTime, which Abby accepted. Pulling over, she watched as he lit a match and began walking toward something that shimmered in the sunlight.

Gasoline.

"No, Derek, don't! Please don't do this!"

But he didn't hear her pleading. She watched in horror as he set the gasoline ablaze, gasoline that would lead straight to Mark's barn.

"I'm sorry," Derek said, although he didn't sound the least bit sorry. "But there was nothing you could do. Goodbye, Abby."

CALEB PULLED out his cell to call 911 while Mark raced to the barn. Harrison shouted after him, but Mark didn't hear him.

Charlie. The horses. They're in there.

When he got closer, he smelled the tell-tale scent of gasoline. He threw open the barn doors, coughing as smoke billowed out.

The fire moved fast as it combined with the gasoline and the dry hay in the barn. Mark heard terrified whinnies of the horses, but no human shouts.

"Charlie? Charlie!" Mark pulled a rag from a nearby hook and covered his mouth, although the smoke burned his eyes. He could still see somewhat; it wouldn't be long before the smoke became impenetrable.

"Charlie!" he screamed.

Then he heard a cry. Mark kept yelling Charlie's name and followed the noise, trying his best to ignore the terrified sounds of the horses.

He used his hands to feel along the stall walls, keeping his bearings, and finally he saw a figure in the corner of one of the stalls. Dropping to his knees, he found Charlie on the ground, already unconscious from the smoke.

"Charlie! Goddammit, Charlie, don't you dare!" Mark slapped his friend, trying to get him to awaken, but Charlie only groaned. Mark forced the panic back. How could he carry Charlie out of here with one arm still only halfway healed? Charlie was a big guy, all muscle, and almost equal to Mark in height.

But Mark had no choice. Grunting with effort, he hauled Charlie's arm around his shoulder, Charlie's dead weight leaning against his good arm. He dropped the rag he'd used to cover his mouth; the smoke filled his mouth and nostrils, burning him and making him cough. Dizziness swamped him.

"Mark! Jesus, Mark!" Caleb rushed into the stall, his face covered with a wet cloth. When he saw Charlie, he swore again. "I'll get him. Get the horses. Harrison can't get near them."

Mark helped Caleb get Charlie to lean on him before getting the horses. He knew which stall contained which horse, and he could almost hear Harrison's voice.

"It won't let me get near it!" Harrison shouted when Mark came into Samson's stall. Samson reared upward, the whites of his eyes showing in the haze.

"Get Rosemary!" Mark shouted. "She's easier. Cover her eyes with a cloth and lead her out. She's the one to the right of this stall."

As Harrison hurried out, Mark worked to calm Samson enough so he could cover his eyes and lead him out. Samson recognized Mark's voice, but he wouldn't let him get close.

With no bridle to grab, Mark was close to panicking, knowing that Delilah and Mirielle were still inside. Finally, Samson let Mark get near him enough to wrap a blindfold around him and lead him outside.

Once they reached the doors and Mark tore off the blindfold, Samson bolted. Mark gasped for air.

Harrison had gotten Rosemary out, and Caleb attended to Charlie, who lay on the ground, still unconscious. But Delilah and Mirielle were still inside. Mark watched as the fire began to lick up the roof, the flames shooting ash and sparks for miles.

He had just enough time to get those two out if he went

fast. Dunking a rag into a nearby pail of water, he rushed into the barn, ignoring his brothers' cries.

The smoke was so bad now that he had to crawl on the ground. His eyes watered, and his lungs seized. He heard Delilah's whinny, and he forced himself to keep going.

He stood up in Delilah's stall and felt her brush up against him. He said her name in soothing tones, and he found Mirielle crouched near her mother.

"There's a good girl." To his relief, Delilah wore a bridle that Charlie must have put on before the fire had started. He didn't know how he'd get both horses out at the same time, but if Mirielle followed Delilah—

"Mark!"

When he heard the voice, he thought he was hallucinating. It couldn't be.

"Abby," he breathed as she burst into the stall. Then: "Abby? What the hell are you doing here?"

"There's no time. I'll take Delilah. Come on!" Her voice was muffled with the rag over her mouth and nose.

Grabbing Delilah's bridle, Abby started to lead the horse out with Mark helping Mirielle. The foal tried to back away into the stall, but Mark was able to wrap an arm around her waist and carry her to safety.

But his bad arm couldn't hold the foal's weight, and he grunted as he began to drop her. He saw Delilah run out the front doors, but he couldn't see Abby now.

"Here!" Abby hurried to his side and helped him carry the foal. His arm screamed, and they'd both be bruised from Mirielle's wicked kicks.

They reached the entrance and set her free, both gasping for breath.

And then only a moment later, a beam began to crash down—right on top of Abby.

ABBY ARRIVED in time to see Mark run into the barn. Caleb and Harrison shouted his name, and Abby couldn't move as she saw the flames engulf the barn. Terror raced through her.

As she'd sped here, she'd called 911, although the dispatch had told her someone else had called minutes earlier. The fire department would be there as soon as they could, but the nearest station was miles away.

And now Mark was inside that burning barn, the stupid man.

"Abby!" Harrison came toward her, covered in soot. "What are you doing here?"

"Mark..." She waited, praying he'd emerge soon. She could barely breathe, and her eyes stung even though she was yards away from the fire.

"He went to get the rest of the horses, the idiot."

She counted to five, then ten, and then she grabbed the rag from Harrison's hand, tied it around her mouth as he watched in astonishment, and sprinted toward the barn.

"Abby! No!"

The heat was so thick that she was sure she'd be burnt alive. Her heart hammered in fear, but when she heard Mark's voice, she moved toward it.

She wasn't going to let him die in this barn. Not before she told him she loved him for a second time. When he saw her, he looked so shocked that she would've laughed. Grabbing

Delilah's bridle, she began to lead the horse from her stall, Mark following with Mirielle.

But once Delilah was free, Abby heard Mark swearing. He was about to drop the foal, who had to weigh at least one hundred pounds, if not more.

Abby wrapped her arms around the foal with Mark holding her from behind, and they awkwardly made their way to the entrance, Mirielle kicking at them every chance she got.

Abby winced as those hooves connected. They were so close, so close—

They set Mirielle on her feet, slapped her rear, and she ran outside.

And then before Abby knew what was happening, she heard Mark scream her name and then a huge weight slammed into her.

Blackness overtook her, her last thought wishing she could've told Mark she loved him.

CHAPTER NINETEEN

Mark heard shouting, but it was from far away. A searing heat ripped into his shoulder, making him gasp and swear. He couldn't see from the smoke, and his lungs struggled for breath.

Abby lay under him, unconscious, and he knew he had to get them out of this damn barn before it was too late.

He tried to push away the beam that had fallen on his left shoulder. Groaning with the effort, he didn't want to touch it with his hands and injure them as well. But the combination of smoke inhalation and his own weak left arm rendered him useless.

"Abby," he muttered, eyes streaming. "Abby, don't leave me. Baby, wake up."

She groaned, but otherwise she didn't stir.

Mark heaved with all of his might, his body screaming in pain everywhere. The beam finally shifted. Yet it wasn't enough to free them.

They were going to die here because he couldn't muster the strength to save the woman he loved.

"Abby, I'm sorry. I'm sorry for everything. I'm an idiot." He didn't know if his eyes were streaming from the smoke or from tears. Maybe both.

"I love you, Abby." His voice was raspy and hoarse, and he coughed until he wheezed.

When Abby's eyes opened a little, he knew he couldn't give up. Not without a fight. He'd die trying to save her, even if it meant his own doom. She was all that mattered now.

He groaned and pushed until he was able to grab the beam with his hands. His palms roared with the pain from the burning wood, but he almost didn't feel it. He was pure adrenaline and resolve. His weak arm screamed at him to stop, and he couldn't see an inch in front of his face with the smoke.

But then the weight lifted off. He gasped at the sensation of freedom, even though his body throbbed from the pain.

There were shouts and voices everywhere, converging upon him, but he couldn't keep his eyes open. The blackness descended and then he knew nothing at all.

ABBY AWOKE to the sound of sirens and water spraying. She smelled smoke, and her throat burned. Rubbing the ash from her eyes, she tried to get her bearings.

"Abby!" Someone called, "She's awake! Abby, what's your last name?"

She shook her head in confusion. "What?"

"What's your last name?" the figure repeated firmly.

"Davison. I need to see—" Mark. *Mark!*

She tried to sit up, but someone pushed her back down.

"He'll be all right. The paramedics are here and they're taking care of him."

Abby realized that it was Caleb who'd pushed her down. Her senses were coming back to her in bits and pieces, and her vision began to clear. She needed something to drink.

"Water," she croaked.

Caleb pressed a bottle into her hand. "Drink up. Can you sit up? Here, let me help you."

She knew she was in shock, and she was more than aware that she'd suffered smoke inhalation. As she came to, she felt herself for any injuries.

She had a burn on her right forearm that had blistered somewhat; her head ached, but when she touched her head for any goose eggs, she didn't find any. More than likely, she'd fainted from the smoke, not from a concussion.

"How is she?" another voice asked. Harrison approached them, looking a little worse for wear.

"I'm okay. I need to see Mark."

She tried to stand up, but she was as wobbly as a newborn foal. That made her think of Mirielle. "The horses?" she gasped.

Harrison helped her stand, his arm around her. "They're okay, although we haven't caught the black one."

"Samson," she whispered.

"Yeah, him. He's a jerk. And Charlie will be all right, too. He collapsed from the smoke."

Right then, a paramedic came up to them and helped Abby get into an ambulance. She looked over her shoulder to watch the firefighters continue to fight the blaze, although she had a feeling the barn was a lost cause. The only good thing was that there were no other buildings near enough to be in danger.

As she was taken to one of the ambulances, she passed one that already had a patient.

Mark!

Crying out, she broke away from her rescuers, ignoring their shouts. She scrambled into the ambulance.

"Ma'am, wait—" a paramedic said, but she brushed him aside.

"I'm a nurse. I'm fine." She collapsed next to Mark, who lay on a stretcher.

He was covered in soot and ash, his eyebrows singed, and his left hand and his shoulder were bandaged. An IV hung overhead, and the paramedic who'd been caring for Mark moved around her to bandage his right hand.

He gazed up at her like he couldn't believe she were real. Choking back a sob, she wanted to touch him, but she was afraid of hurting him. She brushed his hair from his forehead, her tears dripping onto his face.

"You stupid, stupid man," she whispered. "How could you do something so stupid?"

"Who's stupid? You were the one who ran inside a burning building." His voice was a hoarse croak, but Abby laughed anyway.

"Then we're both idiots like your brother said." She wiped her eyes, hiccupping and trying to contain her sobs. "Charlie's going to be okay, and so are the horses. You saved them." Her bottom lip quivered. "You saved me, Mark."

Mark closed his eyes for a moment. When he looked up at her again, those deep green eyes seared through her to her very soul.

"If anyone did the saving, it was you." He touched her fingers with his bandaged left hand. "You saved me, Abby. I wanted to tell you. I love you."

Those words sparked a memory, and she knew without a doubt that he'd said them in the barn earlier. Her tears overflowed now. Kissing his bandaged hand, she wept: from happiness, from terror. But mostly she cried because she loved him so much it hurt.

"I love you, too. You know I do."

He closed his eyes again. "I'll never let you go, Abby." His voice was only a mumble at this point.

"Pain meds," the paramedic explained, blushing a little at being privy to this conversation. "We're going to head to the hospital to get everybody checked out."

"I'll ride with you then."

The paramedic seemed to want to protest, but seeing the resolve in her face, he recognized it wasn't a fight he'd win.

Abby didn't take her eyes off of Mark the entire ride to the hospital.

Two DAYS after he was released from the hospital, Mark grumbled that he was once again laid up with injuries that would prevent him from working.

He'd been lucky, though: no broken bones or life-threatening injuries. He had burns on his hands and on his left shoulder, and a variety of lacerations all over his chest, arms, and back. He also had some large bruises from Mirielle's hooves.

But he didn't mind the pain because everyone had survived.

And Abby—she was alive. She was whole, and well, and the best part?

She loved him still. He loved her, and she hadn't left his side since the fire.

"Lunch is ready," she said as she passed by his bedroom. She stopped when she saw him grimacing. "What is it? Is it your hands?"

He almost wanted to growl at her to stop hovering, but seeing her concerned face stayed his tongue. He was more annoyed with himself than anything else.

"They're fine. Come here." He wrapped her in his arms, resting his chin on top of her head.

They stood like that for a moment, enjoying each other's presence. The sound of their breaths, the beats of their hearts.

Harrison had caught Derek on the edge of Mark's property, and he'd taken him down and dragged him back, kicking and screaming. Caleb to take him into custody, which involved makeshift cuffs involving rope before Caleb had hauled him into the back of his car. Caleb had laughed when he'd admitted that he'd kept Derek in the car by way of child-safety locks.

Derek had been charged with arson, violating his restraining order, and attempted murder, among other crimes. He currently sat in jail, where he would more than likely stay for a very long time.

Charlie had suffered from smoke inhalation, but he had been released from the hospital within a day. He was recuperating at home, his wife driving him crazy by refusing to let him do anything himself. Based on the last phone call he'd had with Mark, he wasn't minding the attention so much.

Both Megan and Sara had reacted with horror, pride, and even a tinge of exasperation upon hearing that their men had decided to play heroes.

Although when they'd heard that Abby had run into a burning barn to help Mark, they'd been so shocked that they'd only gaped at her.

Fiona had come to help at Mark's ranch all day yesterday, but she'd realized that three was a crowd and had left the pair alone. "I'll take care of your cats," she'd told Abby after giving her a hug. "Be sure not to let your young man overwork himself, okay?"

Now, though, Mark murmured into Abby's hair, "I love you." He could never get enough of saying those words. He brushed strands of her brown hair from her face before kissing her.

The kiss deepened without thought, and Abby stood on her tiptoes as Mark delved his tongue inside her mouth. How had he ever thought he could live without her?

She'd saved him—a million times over, and in a million different ways.

"I love you, too," Abby replied a few moments later, her cheeks a little flushed. She bit her lip then, looking away.

He touched her chin. "What is it?"

"I wanted to wait to tell you this, but..." She met his gaze again. "Tina contacted me."

His breath whooshed out of his chest, mostly from surprise. Why would Tina reach out to Abby of all people?

Abby explained, "She heard about the fire, and you being in the hospital. She knew you wouldn't want to talk to her, but she wanted to say that she's sorry for what happened that day and wishes you the best. They both do."

Mark didn't know what to say to that. Oddly enough, he felt nothing at Abby's statement. Neither anger nor gladness.

He'd finally gotten to a place where the past could remain in the past. Because the future only looked brighter and brighter.

"That's nice of her, but can I be honest?" he said.

Abby's lips twitched. "Aren't you usually?"

"Good point." He touched his nose to hers. "I don't care about what Tina says. Or Aaron."

"Really?"

"Really. I hope they have a decent life together with their kid. But I don't want to be a part of it—and that's okay. Because I have you."

Abby's smile grew wider and wider. "Good. Because I don't want to share you with another woman."

"There's no chance in hell of that, baby. You're the only woman I could ever want or need."

They kissed again, this time not parting until they both gasped for air.

After eating lunch, Abby drove them to a neighboring ranch that had offered to house the horses until they could get the barn rebuilt. Mark hated that he couldn't see the horses every day, but all four were being well cared for.

Ranchers in the area had banded together to help Mark run his ranch while he recovered, and it had touched his heart to see the outpouring of support from so many people, many of whom he'd only met a handful of times.

They found all four horses in an outdoor enclosure with a few of the ranch owner's own horses. Mirielle had kept growing, and soon she wouldn't be all legs. The moment Mark approached, Delilah came trotting over to him to nudge him, snorting happily.

"Sorry girl, I didn't bring a carrot for you." He rubbed her nose as best as he could with his bandaged hands. "Are you behaving yourself?"

Mirielle followed her mother and stuck her nose through the gap in the fence, as she wasn't quite tall enough to reach over the top. Abby laughed and kneeled down to give her a good rub.

They entered the enclosure to greet the rest of the horses. The ranch owner, Kevin Wilson, stopped by, and he and Mark chatted for a moment. But Mark only had eyes for Abby as she laughed and talked to the horses, the animals now surrounding her like a band of naughty children.

"I should probably go save her," Mark said when Samson began searching for something to eat in Abby's pockets.

Kevin tipped his hat, grinning. "I think she'll manage."

And she did: Abby gently pushed Samson away, scratching him behind the ears. Mark felt his heart flip over in his chest.

He realized as he walked toward her that Abby had not only saved him, she'd made him a better man. She was *his* miracle, because she'd shown him that love didn't make you a prisoner.

Love could only set you free.

*S*even *months later...*

Abby sneaked out of the room containing the bride and bridesmaids, hoping to find Mark before the ceremony started. Smoothing her bridesmaid's dress down, she did a little preening when she passed a hallway mirror.

Sara had been kind enough to ask her to be in the wedding, and Abby had been more than happy to accept. The extended Thornton clan had embraced Abby, and although Lisa Thornton would always be rather terrifying, she'd accepted Abby in her cool way.

The rest of the family had been as lovely as Abby could've imagined, and she'd gotten closer to Sara, Megan, and even Lizzie, who'd remained in Fair Haven after the New Year.

Abby knew the groomsmen were hiding away in a room somewhere in the palatial Thornton mansion where the ceremony would be held. After Lisa had agreed to keep her involvement in the wedding to a bare minimum, with Harrison exacting a solemn vow that she wouldn't cause Sara even one second of stress, he and Sara had agreed to hold the wedding here.

It was a beautiful place, that was for sure, and now that it was June, the sun shone most days, and flowers bloomed everywhere. A huge purple azalea bush would provide a natural overhang for the ceremony, while hydrangea bushes bursting with color would frame the bride and groom.

But Abby's mind was on other things—and on someone else. When she peeked inside one of the rooms and found no Mark inside, she frowned. Where was he? Knowing him, he was probably hidden away under the stairwell with all of this commotion.

Mark was better about spending time with his family, but he inevitably returned to his ranch to be alone with Abby. "My family is totally crazy," he'd always say in a resigned voice.

"What are you doing out here?" a voice murmured. Then an arm snaked around her waist and pulled her into an empty bedroom.

She laughed breathlessly. "I was looking for you."

"Good answer."

Turning, she let herself appreciate Mark wearing a tuxedo. With his dark hair slicked back and his evergreen eyes gleaming, he was handsomeness incarnate. She smiled as she adjusted his boutonniere.

"I could eat you up right now," she murmured, patting his chest, "but I don't want to mess up your tux."

That made him growl. "Speak for yourself. How long do we have before anyone would notice we were gone?"

"Don't you dare!"

She laughed harder when he pulled her back into his arms and kissed her. She had to wipe lipstick from his face afterward, although luckily he hadn't messed up her very expensive up-do.

"Do you want to tell everyone?" she asked as they sat down together on an armchair, Abby sitting on Mark's lap.

She combed her fingers through his hair; the kissing had disheveled the strands.

"Let's keep it a secret a while longer. Besides, I think upstaging my brother at his wedding would result in me getting punched."

"Good point. Although I'm having a hard time keeping this a secret."

They smiled at each other, and Abby felt the diamond ring hanging between her breasts like a talisman. Mark had proposed to her one night when they'd lain outside under the stars. Although it had been over two weeks since that beautiful night, they hadn't told anyone about the engagement since everyone was preoccupied with Sara and Harrison's wedding.

Sara and Harrison most likely would've been fine with eloping, but they'd both known that the family would've balked, especially with Harrison being the eldest and the first to marry. So they'd agreed to have the whole shebang, and as far as Abby knew, Lisa had kept her nose out of the planning except when necessary. It was her house holding the wedding, after all.

They heard voices, and Abby got up with a sigh. "I think it's time to go." She held out her hand. "Ready?"

Mark took her hand and kissed her fingers. "Always."

They parted when they had to join the bride and groom, smiling at their secret. When Abby entered the large sitting room, she marveled at Sara's transformation. It wasn't so much the gown and the veil—although they were both beautiful—but the glow on her face and the love in her eyes that was infectious.

Sara turned and patted her hair. "Well, what do you think?" she asked.

Along with Abby, Jubilee and Lizzie were bridesmaids, with Megan as the maid of honor. Megan wore her own engagement ring, as Caleb had proposed recently, with the wedding scheduled for the fall.

Lisa and Ruth Flannigan gasped and cooed, while the younger girls all let out breathless sighs at Sara's question.

"You look beautiful," Abby said. She adjusted a flower in Sara's hair. "Harrison is going to fall over when he sees you."

"That's the idea." She grinned. "Where's James?"

"He's with the guys. When he found out that Harrison wasn't allowed to see you before the ceremony, he decided to watch Harrison's every move." Megan's lips twitched. "I think Harrison hasn't even been allowed to go the bathroom without James making sure he doesn't try anything."

That made everyone laugh; even Lisa smiled. Abby had given her future mother-in-law a wide berth, which she would continue to do after she'd married Mark.

Abby didn't want to think about planning a wedding with Lisa hovering. She wondered if Mark would agree to an elopement...

Right before the ceremony began, Megan pulled Abby aside. "You have a secret, and I want to know what it is."

Abby bit her lip. "I do not."

"Liar. You're terrible at it." Megan narrowed her eyes. "Are you pregnant?"

"No!" Abby glanced around. "Don't you dare put that rumor out there! I'd never hear the end of it."

Abby's heart clenched a little at the question. Megan didn't know about Abby's infertility. With Mark's support, though, Abby had begun to stop blaming herself for something she couldn't control.

"Then what is it?" Megan pressed.

Abby unconsciously touched the necklace with her engagement ring hanging from it, the ring hidden from sight in Abby's dress.

Megan, though, wasn't about to let her friend keep a secret for long. She plucked the necklace from Abby's fingers, pulling the ring out of its hiding spot.

"Abby Davison, you sly thing. You got engaged and didn't say a thing? I'm impressed. And disappointed. Why didn't you say anything?"

"Because the wedding was on everybody's minds, and we didn't want to steal Harrison and Sara's thunder." She let Megan inspect the ring before taking it back, hiding it against her heart. "How did you guess I was keeping something?"

"Because you look so happy it's disgusting. You looked like me when Caleb proposed." Megan laughed. "I mean, I'm still disgustingly happy, but there's something about that newly engaged glow, you know?"

"Girls, it's time to go," Lisa said.

"We better get down there. Also, I'm so glad I have you and my sister for support when dealing with our future mother-in-law."

Abby shuddered a little. "Ditto."

Ten minutes later, Abby walked down the aisle with Mark, her heart full to bursting. The sun had begun to set, and it lit the entire ceremony with a golden glow.

Mark squeezed her arm a little before they parted, Abby

standing next to Lizzie at the front, Mark standing next to Caleb. Abby watched as Seth Thornton walked down the aisle with Jubilee.

She'd met Seth at Christmas, but she hadn't seen him since then. He'd gotten leave to attend his oldest brother's wedding, and for the first time since the holidays, all the Thornton siblings were together.

James walked down the aisle after them, looking austere in his duty as ring bearer. According to Sara, he hadn't let the pillow out of his sight, and when he'd been given the rings to carry, he'd vowed that he wouldn't drop them no matter what.

Then the bride's song began, and as the guests stood up, Sara began to walk down the aisle. She looked radiant, and as her gaze caught Harrison's rapt one, Abby's heart fluttered.

No one could deny how much those two adored each other. When Sara reached Harrison, he had to wipe his eyes, which made Sara laugh. Abby saw him mouth the words *I love you*, which she mouthed back.

When the officiant pronounced that Harrison could kiss the bride, Harrison dipped Sara over his arm and kissed her for so long that some of the guests hooted and hollered. Flushing bright red, Sara shook her head before walking back down the aisle with Harrison. The guests cheered and clapped.

Abby found a moment alone with Mark before they had to go take photos. Kissing him so hard that he grunted in surprise, they were panting by the time the kiss ended.

"What was that for?" he asked. "Not that I'm complaining."

"I'm just excited for when it's our turn."

"I couldn't stop thinking about you wearing a beautiful

dress and walking toward me." He kissed her forehead tenderly. "I can't wait for you to be my wife."

"And I can't wait for you to be my husband."

They kissed again, their love overflowing.

"Did you ever imagine this would happen? When you made that deal with me?" she asked.

He smiled. "No, I didn't. I just wanted to be near you. I never thought..." He shook his head. "I didn't know that you would complete me. But I think I fell in love with you that day at The Rise and Shine when you said I was an asshole."

Abby let out a peal of laughter. "I don't know when I fell for you. Maybe it was seeing you with your horses. How much you care for them, how gentle you are with them."

He cleared his throat, looking embarrassed. "Now you're making me blush."

They heard someone calling their names.

"Abby?" he said.

"Yes?"

"I love you. No matter what, I love you."

She smiled. Brushing her nose against his, she whispered, "Same."

LIZZIE THORNTON GAZED at her glass of champagne, wishing she could go hide under the nearest rock. Since her mother wasn't particularly fond of large boulders in her backyard, Lizzie wondered if she could hide in the bushes instead.

Lisa would love that, finding her daughter hiding in the shrubbery.

The reception continued into the night, with guests dancing, drinking, and having a grand time. The bride and groom danced like lovestruck idiots. It was sweet, Lizzie knew, but she felt a pang in her heart looking at them.

She felt a pang looking at all three of her older brothers. They'd all found love, hadn't they? Caleb and Megan, newly engaged; Mark and Abby, soon-to-be engaged, if she had to bet. The only small consolation was that her twin brother Seth was as single as she was, and Jubilee? Well, Jubilee was a baby, wasn't she?

Wait, how old was her sister now? Twenty-three? Twenty-four?

Lizzie pushed her champagne glass away. She'd already drunk too much. Now she was getting pathetic, and she refused to be pathetic. She was genuinely happy for Harrison and Sara. She wouldn't begrudge them their joy.

If she were hung up on a certain asshole ex—an asshole ex who was here at this wedding—well, that was her problem. No reason to kill the mood because she couldn't get over something. Or someone.

Someone placed a glass of water in front of her, and then Seth sat down across from her without a word. Once upon a time, she and Seth had been a frightful duo. They'd had a bond only other twins could understand, and they'd once been able to finish each other's sentences.

But after Seth had joined the Marines and Lizzie had run off to be a musician, they'd lost that closeness. Lizzie wished they could find it again.

This Seth, she had to admit, was a stranger to her. Solemn, quiet, there was a darkness that lurked in his gaze. She didn't even want to imagine the things he'd seen while overseas. If Mark was closed-off, Seth was robotic. He'd stuffed his emotions so far down that Lizzie wasn't sure anyone could find them, least of all Seth.

She sipped her water. Seth knew what she needed still, didn't he? Lizzie was technically older than him, but in some ways, he'd been the older one. He'd been the responsible one, the mature one. He'd known what to do.

Her throat closed. *No, don't. Don't go back to that place.*

She forced a smile. "You don't want to dance?"

They both watched as Caleb did some form of the chicken dance, Megan looking on in embarrassment. The twins gave each other *the look.*

"I'm good," Seth replied, deadpan. "What about you? Don't musicians dance?"

She scoffed. "I'm not a pop star. And do you see these heels?" She pointed her toe at him, showing him her stilettos. "No way I'm dancing."

"That's a shame," a voice rumbled behind her, "because I was just about to ask you to dance."

Lizzie wondered if this was a movie, because it felt like she was watching one. Like she'd separated from her body, and she was watching someone else turn and gaze upon the man who'd haunted her for so long.

This person she barely knew, who'd grown from an earnest kid to a hardened man, all angles and swirling tattoos. Wearing a suit that only showed how his shoulders had broadened over the years, Trent Younger possessed a kind of handsomeness that intimidated.

Or maybe it was the tattoos. They were mostly hidden, although a few curled around his throat above the collar of his shirt. On anyone else it would look excessive, but on Trent?

It made Lizzie's mouth water.

Seth glanced between them, his eyes narrowed. If Trent was intimidating, Seth was terrifying. And the last thing Lizzie needed was these two males going at it like some kind of cock fight. Seth had disliked Trent for years.

"I'll dance with you," Lizzie said. "But if I step on your toes, don't get mad."

She held out her hand, like a dare, and Trent smiled as he enclosed her fingers in his. She refused to notice how her heart pounded, or how she wished she could bury her nose in Trent's suit jacket and inhale his spicy scent.

The band played a slow song, and as Trent put his arm around her waist, she focused on the song itself. *Standard time signature, key is A minor,* she thought to herself as she dissected the musical notes. She winced a little when the oboe began. *He's really flat. Did he tune at all?*

She focused on music whenever reality became too pressing. Like now. With Trent holding her, his warmth and his scent flooding her, she struggled to keep her bearings. She'd lose herself in him, lose herself in the memories.

How was it that he seemed so different, and yet exactly the same?

They'd had a whirlwind love affair their senior year of high school, falling so hard and fast for each other that it had been dizzying. Lizzie had thought he was the love of her life for a time.

But life never liked to work out like you expected.

"Are you in town for long?" Trent murmured. His eyes gleamed from the soft lights hanging overhead. "Or are you going back on the road soon?"

"I'll be here for the summer. I needed a break." *And I think my muse has dried up,* she thought.

They didn't speak after that, drifting to the music. Lizzie focused on the violinist, who played his instrument with an emotion she couldn't identify. It seemed tinged with sadness. Loss? Had he lost someone recently?

"So it's going to be like this, is it?" Trent said quietly, his breath heating her ear. "We're going to avoid each other and act like neither of us exists?"

She flinched. Catching his gaze, she struggled with a reply. "What do you want me to say?"

"I don't know, Lizzie. You tell me."

Her head was starting to pound, and her feet hurt, and she really didn't need this right now. She walked away, not caring that people were watching. She heard Trent swear as he followed her.

He always did that—followed her when she didn't want him to.

He tugged her around the corner of the house, where darkness gave them cover. She wanted to push him away, but at the same time, she wanted to wrap herself around him. How could he upset her balance after all of this time?

She wanted to be free of him—once and for all.

"Leave me alone, Trent," she said dully. "Please."

"Do you think I want this? I haven't seen you for three years, but it's like no time has passed."

He touched her cheek, but she turned away.

"Please." Her voice was a plea. Her throat thickened with tears. "I can't do this."

"Can't we at least be friends? Or polite acquaintances?"

So much flooded back to her—memories, images, sounds, emotions—and she couldn't catch her breath. He was right, though: it was like no time had passed at all. Maybe because in a way, neither of them had dealt with what had happened.

She swallowed. "I need to go." She pushed past him, stumbling, her heels getting caught in the soft grass.

Trent said her name and before she could go tumbling onto the ground, he caught her again.

"Dammit, Lizzie, you always do this. You always run away."

"And you always follow me! You won't leave me alone. I want to be alone." She wanted to hurt him; she wanted to scream at him.

She wanted to touch him; embrace him; kiss him—until nothing else mattered.

"Do you really want to be alone? Be honest for once. I know you better than anyone." He was a whisper away, his smell making her dizzy again.

"Yes. I do," she lied.

He laughed, low and almost sadly. "I wish I could leave you alone. It's my only wish. I've tried to move on, and yet—"

She could just make out his grimace in the low light. He let go of her arm, but it was only to cup her face in his calloused palm. He brushed his thumb along her cheek.

"I'm going to kiss you," he murmured.

Her mouth parted. The sounds in the distance faded away, because now all she could hear was the sound of her heart beating in time with Trent's.

She breathed him in. And then she replied in a whisper, "Yes."

ABOUT THE AUTHOR

A coffee addict and cat lover, Iris Morland writes sexy and funny contemporary romances. If she's not reading or writing, she enjoys binging on Netflix shows and cooking something delicious.

www.ingramcontent.com/pod-product-compliance
Lightning Source LLC
Chambersburg PA
CBHW050356190726
48284CB00007BB/2313